# THE FORGOTTEN AND THE FANTASTICAL 5

# Also by Teika Bellamy

**Editor:**

*Musings on Mothering* (Mother's Milk Books 2012)
*Letting Go* by Angela Topping (Mother's Milk Books 2013)
*Look at All the Women* by Cathy Bryant (Mother's Milk Books 2014)
*The Mother's Milk Books Writing Prize Anthology 2013: PARENTING* (Mother's Milk Books 2014)
*The Forgotten and the Fantastical* (Mother's Milk Books 2015)
*Hearth* by Sarah James and Angela Topping (Mother's Milk Books 2015)
*Oy Yew* by Ana Salote (Mother's Milk Books 2015)
*The Mother's Milk Books Writing Prize Anthology 2014: THE STORY OF US* (Mother's Milk Books 2015)
*Echolocation* by Becky Cherriman (Mother's Milk Books 2016)
*The Forgotten and the Fantastical 2* (Mother's Milk Books 2016)
*Maysun and the Wingfish* by Alison Lock (Mother's Milk Books 2016)
*Handfast* by Ruth Aylett and Beth McDonough (Mother's Milk Books 2016)
*Baby X* by Rebecca Ann Smith (Mother's Milk Books 2016)
*The Mother's Milk Books Writing Prize Anthology 2015: LOVE* (Mother's Milk Books 2016)
*The Forgotten and the Fantastical 3* (Mother's Milk Books 2017)
*Nondula* by Ana Salote (Mother's Milk Books 2017)
*Inheritance* by Ruth Stacey and Katy Wareham Morris (Mother's Milk Books 2017)
*Spools of Thread* by Angi Holden (Mother's Milk Books 2018)
*The Forgotten and the Fantastical 4* (Mother's Milk Books 2018)
*Nigma* by Ana Salote (Mother's Milk Books 2019)

# THE FORGOTTEN AND THE FANTASTICAL 5

Modern fables and ancient tales

EDITED BY TEIKA BELLAMY

Mother's Milk Books

First published in Great Britain in 2019 by Mother's Milk Books

Cover image 'Beyond the Pale' copyright © Jessica Shirley 2018
Cover design copyright © Teika Bellamy 2019
Introduction copyright © Teika Bellamy 2019
Illustrations copyright © Emma Howitt 2019

Copyright of the stories resides with individual authors.

ISBN 978-1-9162437-0-5

All rights reserved. No part of this book may be reproduced, stored in a retrieval system, or transmitted in any form, or by any means, electronic, mechanical, photocopying, recording or otherwise, without prior written permission from the copyright holders as listed on this page and on pages 193–198.

Typeset in Georgia, Lt Oksana and Old Newspaper Types
by Teika Bellamy.
Lt Oksana font designed by Lauren Thompson,
Old Newspaper Types font designed by Manfred Klein.
Printed and bound in Great Britain by Imprint Digital, Devon.
https://digital.imprint.co.uk

First published in 2019 by Mother's Milk Books
www.mothersmilkbooks.com

## SPECIAL THANKS TO:

My amazing family who continue to support
all my creative endeavours.
My co-editor and friend, Helen Lloyd,
who is always there to lend a hand.
Molly Llewellyn for proofreading.
Emma Howitt and Jessica Shirley for their gorgeous artwork.
The wonderful writers who continue
to be bewitched by the bewitching.
And all those who believe in me and Mother's Milk Books,
especially M.

# CONTENTS

| | | |
|---|---|---|
| Introduction | TEIKA BELLAMY | 9 |
| Pelt | ANGELA READMAN | 11 |
| The Glass Legs (or, it's easier than you think) | KATIE GRAY | 21 |
| People Will Talk | DONNA M DAY | 41 |
| The White Wolf | SARAH HINDMARSH | 47 |
| Princess, Star, Brilliant | ROSIE GARLAND | 53 |
| Fossils | BECKY CHERRIMAN | 59 |
| Human Point-oh | JONTY LEVINE | 69 |
| The Fox's Wedding | CARYS CROSSEN | 75 |
| Dark Glass | LOUISE M M RICHARDS | 91 |
| My Son, My Daughter | KERIS MCDONALD | 97 |
| The Glass Slipper | KIM GRAVELL | 107 |
| Darling Grace | NOEL CHIDWICK | 117 |
| Chantress | ALIYA WHITELEY | 135 |
| The Art Glass Paperweight | MARIJA SMITS | 149 |
| Notes on Stories | | 163 |
| Index of Writers with Biographies | | 193 |

# INTRODUCTION

Whenever Mother's Milk Books opens to submissions for *The Forgotten and the Fantastical* anthologies I never know what kind of stories I'm going to get. It's always fascinating to see what themes have been simmering away in the writers' collective consciousness, brought forth into story form. This year, wolves, beauty, enchanted glass and what it means to be human – indeed, what reality itself is – were all themes that emerged, along with the perennial topic of women seeking out a better life. That made choosing the stories for this year's collection relatively straightforward. What I particularly like about *The Forgotten and the Fantastical 5* is that the stories of new authors sit comfortably alongside those of established and well-known authors. No matter how experienced we are in writing, when it comes to the human psyche, we all have a story to tell. I hope very much that you, dear reader, will connect with the stories within.

**Teika Bellamy, Autumn 2019**

# Pelt

by

Angela Readman

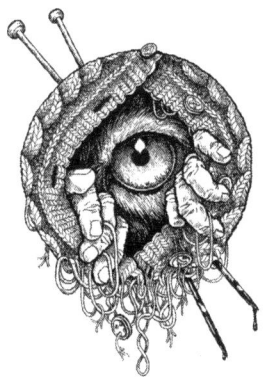

## **Pelt**

I wasn't myself when they gave me the finger. I reeked of liver and spit. I'd been lathered in the aroma since they dragged me out of the wolf. Or, at least, I felt I had. I was certain I stank, though nobody said anything. When they came to see me, no one talked about what happened at all, though I knew the village spoke of little else. Gasping, they savoured each juicy detail. The girl. The red cape. The woodsman, his perfume of sawdust and pine. The glint of his axe.

Wolf skins swayed in the market square, strung between the stalls like bunting. 'Small mercies,' women whispered, clutching their babies, 'it could have been us.' Their husbands slapped one another's backs outside the inn, daring any wolf to show its furry face around here. Oh, they'd show them, all right. They were ready. They had weapons. Traps had been set. Children wound around their parents' legs wearing pointed ears on their heads. So many wolves had been killed lately, the tanner made the scrap fur on their heads into hats.

I crept through the crowd and bought chicken livers and oxtail. Shoving the meat under my coat, I sloped past a bunch of boys taking turns to hold THE axe. So small, considering the damage it did. Little girls dared each other to stroke the blade and squealed like fireworks. I winced, the hairs on my neck standing on end. The world had got pointy since I stepped out of the wolf, every sound was so sharp.

The path was alive with falling leaves. I heard rabbits and mice scuffle through the undergrowth and snuck into the forest in the same spot as always, turning to check no one was following. The sun was rose-gold. It lacked the brassiness of summer, yet when I stepped out of the canopy of the trees, an hour later, wiping my slimy fingers on my skirt, I had to hold my hand over my eyes. I squinted. The sky was rosy and raw looking as something skinned. The world was such a dazzling place now, it hurt. I couldn't stay out in it for long, I scurried on. The girl would already be on her way to the cottage. I found visitors liked to find me exactly where they left me.

I let myself in, dropping the key by the door. For a moment, I fought the strangest urge to knock. It didn't seem quite the same as it was, though it all appeared the same. The broom leaned against the wall. The jug sat on the mantel, pale and empty as a swan. I poked the fire and the flames snatched the log. I sat and got up. Sat, and got up. Rubbing my arms to keep warm. Ever since the wolf, I felt freezing no matter what I wore.

I can only compare the feeling to those first nights of being widowed. After people had left with their fruit cake and stodgy condolences, I'd crawl into bed and roll into the absence. The depression on my husband's side of the mattress felt like a sculpture it took forty years to carve. Touching it, I was so cold it seemed a blizzard stormed inside me and all I could do was knit a shawl. It was the same after the wolf. I couldn't stop snapping kindling and scrubbing the floor. I kept busy, busy, busy to bury one icy thought I couldn't shake. That it took just a second for something to swallow me whole. Gulp. I was there, then gone.

The blackberries straggling the footpath snapped with a crack. I grabbed the knitting and lay it across my lap, to please my granddaughter. I knew it was her. I'd know her footsteps anywhere. Though lately, her footsteps sounded so much cockier than they once did. Of course, they were. She'd skipped out of the claws of a wolf. There wasn't a fang or claw in the forest, not for her.

The door flew open and she breezed in. It was windy,

orange leaves skittered across the stone floor and lay still. She unburdened her basket one item at a time and listed the contents out loud, as if I was too stupid to know anything I'm not told. *Blackcurrant jam, sausages, a cut of venison, yesterday's eggs, with a feather still clinging to the shell.* 'Look, I brought you those sausages you like,' she said.

'Lovely,' I said, 'very nice.' I knew what the basket contained before she'd even finished emptying it. I could smell it. I could smell everything ever since the wolf. I was pulled out like something freshly born. I sniffed out the girl's soap, the lone alpine strawberry she popped between her lips on her way here. And even the pine off the woodcutter's hands that held hers just last night, under a stingy moon outside her mother's house. I breathed in the life of a seventeen-year-old girl until my eyes watered and pretended I couldn't smell the herbs in the sausages. Sage is the devil's work. I liked my meat rare.

'How are you today?' she asked. 'Shall I cook you a snack?' She peered into the pantry, swaying on the door like a dance partner. 'Did you finish that mutton already? And the lamb? Hmm. Let's see, how about some jam on toast?'

The jam was so dark the firelight struggled to peek through the jar. I pushed it away across the table. I've never cared for jam, if I'm honest. I have a saltier tooth. I'd told people before. They kept bringing it anyway. Lately, I carried whole jars to the forest and smeared it on tree trunks for the wasps to get drunk.

'I'm not hungry,' I said.

She sat and began the chore of keeping me company, chatting about her father, the stag he shot, the woodsman — who wanted to marry so soon, and her mother's advice to give it a while. Wait and see what's love and what's gratitude.

'Lovely. It will all work out fine.' I said what she expected a grandma to say. I had a few sentences I spoke in her presence, nothing more.

'How are you managing without your glasses?' she asked, 'Can you see?'

We stared at the silver frames on the mantel, the cracked lenses webbed with firelight. I'd never seen so clearly in my life. I saw so vividly now it hurt, like walking into sunlight when you've been in the dark.

'I get by,' I muttered, 'mustn't grumble.'

She looked at me and I recalled fur. When I was inside the wolf, I looked out and saw my life through a small wound in its pelt. I had seen her moving around, so carefully, filling my water, tending the wildflowers in the jug. I saw how she'd perched by the bed and folded her hands on her knee, afraid to touch me lest my brittle bones snap.

Now, she glanced at the stump where the axe had clipped my hand. The scar smooth as the skin under a wedding band. The finger was gone.

'Does it hurt?' she whispered.

'No.'

'What *does* it feel like?'

'Nothing,' I said. Except, sometimes, I'd catch sight of my hand and feel it wasn't really mine. It wasn't so different to seeing my face in a window. The old woman there bore no resemblance to how I felt inside.

'It's so quiet.' She inspected the cape I'd promised to make her. Darker red this time. Less prone to stain. 'You've been stuck on the same row forever.' I watched her fidget with the wool and wondered if she missed the sound of my knitting. The soothing click of needles, constant as a clock. She probably never noticed it until it was gone.

'Thinking about it, I never see you knit or sew these days. You're different,' she said, 'Quieter. Is your finger bothering you?'

'Yes,' I said, to stop her staring at me, 'that's all that's bothering me, stitching the hours away doesn't come as easily.'

'You'll get used to it,' her face lit up, 'You'll adapt. People do. You'll be right as rain in no time! Come on, give me a smile.'

I smiled like my teeth were in a glass and waited for her to go.

In the morning, I rushed through the forest clutching the venison, looking behind me every few paces. I kept my eyes peeled for hare skin on the forest floor. I saw feathers, the bones of birds, and I grinned at the carnage. I placed the meat on the ground and listened to crows breaking out from the trees. Rabbits hot-footed it to their burrows. The undergrowth shivered as the wolves nosed out of their den.

There were five pups when I found them. Four survived. Gangly, scrawny and not long weaned. They nosed out looking for their mother as if they could still remember being blind. The day after I was sliced out of her, I felt pulled to the forest. I wandered through the trees searching for something I couldn't name. Then, I saw them. The cubs. Hungry, wary, wild, fur like burnt out fires on snow. They needed me.

One was always bolder than the others. He snatched the meat and darted off with it now, his brothers and sisters sidling in for their share. I took a step towards the pack. They bared their teeth and snarled, barely needing me now. My heart leapt. I felt alive.

Bacon, mutton, pheasant, raven pie, I had fed the wolves whatever I could. I saw their teeth grow and finally knew they could survive the winter without me, yet I still came. Looking around, I pictured someone following me and wondered what would happen if anyone discovered what I was doing. The hunters wouldn't like it. There'd be consequences. Raised voices. Pointing. Currently, the mood in the village was: wolves are for killing, any other opinion is a betrayal.

They pounded at my door on Friday afternoon. I froze with the broom in my hand. The footsteps outside weren't friends. I heard shuffling, stomped undergrowth, the stamp of a heel. My granddaughter wasn't alone. I lifted the latch and braced myself to face the onslaught of furious neighbours. I'd always known this day would come. I was almost disappointed it took so long.

'It's alright it's just us!' the girl said. My daughter in-law, the woodcutter, and the local blacksmith huddled around my door. 'Look, what we've got for you. He made it. Isn't he clever!' The blacksmith blushed as the girl handed me something wrapped in cloth and string. I wound it free and stared at a hollow metal tube, unsure what it was.

'It's a finger! You'll be able to sew again,' the girl said, 'Go on, try it on.'

I stood still, not moving until they held out the finger and showed me how it tied on. Their faces shone with anticipation. The stump didn't find its way into the copper sleeve as smoothly as they'd hoped. I looked at them and saw they'd imagined I'd see it and slip it on instantly, recognise it as mine like a hand knows the right glove.

'It's perfect! Try it out. Pick up the kettle. Pick up that book, your sewing box. That's right!'

I moved around my house following their instructions. I picked up the kettle, opened a book, found a spoon and moved it in and out of a bowl. I clutched my knitting and purled a stitch, the metal fingertip clicking against the needles. I finally sat by the fire, one hand dangling over the chair arm. The visitors cheered. 'Hurray! It works wonders. You can do everything just like before.' They crowded around me awaiting an appropriate reaction. Tears. Joy. Gratitude, anything.

'I don't know what to say,' I said. Lovely. Good. Very nice.

'You look like your old self again,' the girl said, 'see, good as new.'

She went to hold my hand and dropped it. I was sitting so close to the fire the copper had conducted the heat of the flame and the fingertip seared her palm. There was a blister on her palm, the blossoming of raw skin, a small burn. I took her hand and licked it.

'We'd better be going,' she pulled away, startled for a second before she resumed a bright smile. And they say a wolf has a mask on its face. 'You need your rest,' she said.

I watched her bring her burnt hand to her mouth and drop it on her way to the door, pretending it didn't hurt, insisting everything was back to being the same as it always was.

I waved at the visitors until they had gone, my finger flashing in the falling light. I laughed along with them, knowing I would never be the same as I was.

I had been inside the wolf. No one has ever asked how it was, but I wished someone would. It was like being held by arms so strong you believe they'll never let go. In the dark, under that silver pelt, all I could hear was a heart, fiercely beating, pressed against my own.

# The Glass Legs
# (or, it's easier than you think)

by

Katie Gray

# The Glass Legs
# (or, it's easier than you think)

'They are made of glass.' With a glance towards the house, Cordelia hitched up her skirt and showed Audrey a delicate, translucent ankle.

'Glass?' Audrey echoed, not quite believing the evidence of her own eyes. Cordelia's ankle flexed and bent almost as flesh. It had a smoky quality, a hint of creamy-yellow, like champagne. Audrey could see the lawn through Cordelia's ankle, warped and tinted.

'Papa's idea,' said Cordelia. 'You see – well I suppose you've heard, about what happened. Everyone has.'

Audrey had heard of the accident, though perhaps not through the usual channels. The quarrel with her father. The ill-fated ride, alone, into the countryside. The fall. The broken legs. The heat of the day. The long hours that had passed before she was found.

Cordelia had not been seen in the public eye for a year. Word in the city had been that both her legs had been cut off by the physician to save her life. That she had died of shock and loss of blood. That she was bedbound. That her mind had been broken as well as her body. That she would never be seen again.

Cordelia had returned, unharmed, with dainty footsteps and a dipped glance.

'They're strong enough to walk on,' said Cordelia. 'But you see, if I'm too rough they might crack or shatter.'

'No more riding?' said Audrey.

'No more anything.' Cordelia let her skirt fall to cover her glass ankle. 'And of course one word from Papa and they seize up. I am like a statue. But no matter,' she said, and smiled. 'They are better than nothing.'

Audrey's stomach turned.

\*

Despite what people often supposed, it was easy. A change of clothes and the right attitude and you could get in anywhere. Audrey had begun pronouncing her name *Smythe* instead of *Smith* and introducing herself as 'Mister'. A change of a single sound in her first name, a D to a B. As yet no one had questioned her.

Mr Aubrey Smythe, a young gentleman whose father, now deceased, had lost the family fortune in unwise investments. It was a story that touched a lot of hearts. It was a story that opened a lot of doors. And who she had been before she was Mr Aubrey Smythe? Did it really matter?

In Sir Montgomery's smoking room she lolled back in an armchair, watching the cigar smoke curl towards the yellowed ceiling, listening with one ear to the conversation. She never truly relaxed in the company of men, but she would make herself comfortable nonetheless.

'So what is it you do, then?' said one of the other guests.

He was a young man with a pointed beard and straight away Audrey had pegged him as a sorcerer. He had a certain swagger about him, a powerful swagger that only sorcerers and the exceptionally wealthy had. He wasn't well-dressed enough to be exceptionally wealthy; hence, he was a sorcerer. Looking to find a patron in the lord of the house, most likely.

She took a long, confident drag on her cigar and said, 'My family owns land in the East.'

'Ah,' he said, nodding, and she could see him thinking, *layabout*. 'Mr Smythe, was it?'

'That's right,' she said.

'Mr Chuffley.' He extended his hand.

What an absurd name for a sorcerer, *Chuffley*. 'Are you an apprentice?'

She had meant to embarrass him, for he looked old enough

to be a trained sorcerer, but he said, 'Yes, actually. Why? Know any magic yourself?'

'None at all,' said Audrey.

There was a soft knock upon the door, so soft that Audrey was sure her keen ears were the only ones to hear it. Cordelia's sweet and pretty face peered inside.

'Ah, Cordelia!' boomed Sir Montgomery over the raucous chatter of his guests. 'To what do we owe the pleasure?'

'I'm taking an early night, papa,' said Cordelia.

'Oh, yes, yes.' Sir Montgomery beckoned her over. 'You rest – come and give me a kiss.'

Cordelia obligingly kissed her papa's bald, glistening head, waved goodnight to the assembled gentlemen, and walked in dainty, measured steps to the door.

'I tell you,' said Mr Chuffley as the door closed, speaking softly, so as not to be heard by certain parties. 'Whoever wins *her* hand will be the envy of the kingdom.'

Audrey said, 'Yes. A real treasure.'

\*

'Well, at any rate, papa doesn't like me to talk about it,' said Cordelia. 'He says it was for the best.'

'For the best?' Audrey's tone was sharp and her voice high. She was too outraged to keep it low in her chest.

'He says losing my legs made a lady of me.'

Forgetting herself Audrey said, 'I can imagine nothing worse.'

Cordelia gave her a look that she had given to men herself, once upon a time. *You can't possibly understand this.* And in truth, she couldn't. A woman she might be, but she had never been a lady.

'Mr Smythe,' she pronounced, 'you are a *most* peculiar gentleman.'

'That I am,' Audrey agreed.

'Would you care to take a turn about the lake?' Rising from her stone seat, Cordelia adjusted her skirts, ensuring that her glass limbs were fully covered. 'It's lovely.'

'Would your papa approve?' said Audrey, she hoped with a touch of wit.

'Certainly not,' said Cordelia in curt tones. 'He thinks you a layabout – if an amusing one. But you are a guest in my house and I have a responsibility to entertain you.'

Audrey smiled and offered her arm. Cordelia, dipping her gaze, accepted it.

They walked on along the path, Cordelia's parasol neatly over her shoulder, her gloved hand upon Audrey's arm. Audrey's heart quickened in a way it hadn't in a long time.

'Are they... easy to walk on?' She eyed Cordelia's feet as they emerged, one at a time, from beneath the arch of her hoop skirt.

'Stiff,' said Cordelia. 'Always as if I haven't used them in weeks. I still feel as an invalid.'

Ordinarily Audrey had no interest in matters of sorcery but something about Cordelia's glass legs fascinated her even as she was repelled. She might have asked more questions, but refrained, for they were Cordelia's legs and she was, for the present, a gentleman.

'How long do you mean to stay in my father's house?' said Cordelia.

'As long as he'll have me,' said Audrey. She said it lightly, as if it were a joke, but meant it most sincerely.

'Good,' said Cordelia with a fierce kind of earnestness. 'This way – through the rose garden.'

The roses smelled sweet and the sun overhead had grown bright. Cordelia stopped to look at the blossoms, a slight smile crossing her face.

Past the trellis, the lake. Audrey smelled it before she saw it. A cool, green expanse of water, deep and dark, hung about with trailing willow trees. She ached to swim in it, as she had swum in the lakes and rivers at home in the North.

'I used to swim here,' Cordelia remarked.

'No swimming now?' said Audrey.

'None whatsoever,' said Cordelia. 'But I like to come here. Tis a beautiful spot. I'm glad you joined me, Mr Smythe.'

Audrey said, 'As am I.'

\*

Summer, of course, was the season of balls and social gatherings. The circle of guests in Sir Montgomery's house would swell and ebb as the season continued. Beautiful ladies and handsome gentlemen, counts and knights and barons, businessmen and sorcerers

Mr Chuffley wasn't one for balls. In the evening, while the beautiful ladies and handsome gentlemen were dancing, Audrey found him on the veranda with his half-swilled drink, moody. Perhaps he had hoped his sorcery would give him some sway with the ladies. But he was short, rotund, sweaty, and sorcery could only take one so far.

Many of the ladies had looked at Audrey with bright, inviting eyes. She asked one or two to dance before slipping away, for appearances. Ordinarily she would have delighted in such an occasion but her own eyes were ever drawn to Cordelia, and Cordelia did not leave her seat.

'What do you know about glass?' she said to Mr Chuffley.

Mr Chuffley blinked in astonishment behind his spectacles. 'Pardon me?' he said. 'Sir, I am a sorcerer, not a common glassblower.'

There was nothing *common* about glassblowing but

Audrey didn't comment. 'Glass,' she said. 'Its uses in magic.'

'Ah,' he said. 'Numerous and tedious. Why do you ask? Have you considered reading a book?'

'I prefer to ask questions,' said Audrey. 'How much do you know about working magic with glass?'

Mr Chuffley sighed, and pushing up his spectacles rubbed a hand across his tired eyes. But perhaps he realised this was the most fun he was going to have all evening. 'As much as I care to know,' he said. 'Glass is a man-made material, and thus is easy to enchant.'

'Do you know,' said Audrey, 'about Cordelia's legs?'

Mr Chuffley sputtered. 'Her legs?'

Audrey had considered how it might sound, *her legs*, but she hadn't been able to think of a better way to ask and so had decided to be blunt. 'You must have heard the story.'

'That she lost them? Yes. A patent untruth, or else she wouldn't bally well be walking.'

'Her legs are made of glass,' said Audrey. 'Do you know how such a thing might be done?'

'I – glass?' Mr Chuffley gaped at her, then with a sniff composed himself. 'Don't be absurd. You couldn't possibly make an artificial limb from glass. It would break.'

'So you don't know,' said Audrey.

'I didn't say that,' said Mr Chuffley. 'I, I don't imagine it would be impossible. Few things are, with magic. But I dare say it would be highly inadvisable. Whatever makes you think they're made of glass?'

'She told me.' She refrained from saying *she showed me*, that being a remark that more likely than not would find its way back to Cordelia's father.

'Good gracious.' Mr Chuffley's round face had become a touch pink. 'I'm, I'm sure she was being fanciful. Gels, you know.'

'She was telling the truth,' said Audrey. 'Her legs are made of glass.'

'How impractical,' said Mr Chuffley.

'I rather think that's the point.'

'Ah.' Mr Chuffley toyed with his wine glass, casting yellowish shadows upon his face as he turned it and turned it. She could see him working it out, see the wheels spinning in his transparent face. 'Well. Hm.'

He didn't like it. She could tell it made him uneasy – more than uneasy. There was something about the whole affair that revolted him but he couldn't say so, certainly not in as many words, without suggesting that their gracious host, his potential patron, might perhaps have done something he oughtn't.

Or perhaps he didn't understand why it revolted him.

'Do you know how such a thing might be done?' said Audrey.

'Why do you want to know?' said Mr Chuffley in stiff tones.

'Intellectual curiosity,' said Audrey.

'A very complex enchantment, I'm sure,' said Mr Chuffley. 'If you'll excuse me, I think I hear someone calling me.'

Audrey caught him by the arm. He looked at her, face pinkening once again, deeply affronted. 'Mr Chuffley, sir, may I be frank with you?'

'Frank?' said Mr Chuffley. 'Well, er, yes.'

'Cordelia tells me her father has some hold over her – over her legs, I mean. She says he can control the enchantment. How might such a thing be done?'

Mr Chuffley stared at her, his eyes very big and owlish behind those ridiculous spectacles. He might perhaps not see through her. Or he might understand and be willing to collude, if only for a few moments. She thought those the most likely possibilities. If he instead decided to tell Lord Montgomery the questions she had asked, she'd be sunk.

He took his arm from hers. 'Intellectual curiosity?' he said.

'Idle intellectual curiosity,' said Audrey. 'I haven't a whit of magic myself and I doubt his lordship does either. I'm intrigued.'

'Yes, quite.' Adjusting his collar, Mr Chuffley went on. 'Well, ah, for someone who isn't himself a sorcerer – to control a spell, he would need some kind of charm, or talisman.'

'I see,' said Audrey. 'What might it be like?'

'It might be anything,' said Mr Chuffley. 'Anything at all. Now, if you'll excuse me.'

Pushing past her, he blundered through the French windows to the stifling atmosphere of the dance.

\*

Once upon a time, when Audrey was a girl of twelve, she had gone by the name of Tommy. As Tommy she'd had various jobs, chief amongst them delivering messages, but she'd turned her hand now and again to selling charms.

Her charms, which she'd bought from the girls who peddled in the seamstress district and then sold up on the hilltops to those rich enough to afford it but not so rich as to know better, had been made of string and beads and stones that looked semi-precious. Her amulets had been carved rocks and pieces of worked wood.

What a real amulet or charm or talisman looked like? She hadn't the first idea.

She returned to the party and found Cordelia in a plush seat by a window, watching the sedate dances, her face glowing. Her head swayed gently in time with the music, back and forth, and Audrey saw the toe of one neat slipper, just visible beneath her skirt, tapping from side to side.

Mustering all her courage, Audrey stepped to Cordelia's side and offered her hand. 'Care to dance?'

Cordelia's daze dipped at once, and that hint of slipper vanished. It was not, Audrey suspected, a display of genuine demurity; it was that the question saddened her. 'Oh, no, sir, I cannot,' she said. 'I'm a dreadful dancer.'

'That's not what I've heard.' As it happened, Audrey hadn't heard a thing about Cordelia's dancing but it was a fair bet, that once upon a time she had been graceful.

Cordelia's eyes rose and for a moment they had a wistful, faraway look in them. Then they turned cross. 'Well sir, you heard incorrectly. I do not dance.'

'That's a pity,' said Audrey. 'Being as this is your own party. Are you sure you mightn't try?'

Cordelia bit her lip and said nothing.

'I shan't ask again,' said Audrey. She dropped her hand.

But as she stepped away Cordelia rose to her feet with a practiced and delicate grace. 'One dance,' she said. 'Then I shall retire.'

'One dance,' Audrey echoed, and taking Cordelia's hand she led her out into the hall.

She had never learned any of these noble dances, but she had watched, and she learned quickly by watching. Holding Cordelia's hand high she joined the line of gentlemen as it ambled down the hall.

Cordelia took a step beside her, and another, her movements slow but not ungraceful. On the third step she stumbled and winced so painfully that Audrey had half a mind to call the dance off. But then Cordelia straightened, and brightened. Holding up her head she gripped Audrey's hand tighter, and the dance began.

When first Audrey turned her, Cordelia stumbled, tottering as one wearing stilts. She regained her composure quickly and said as they switched hands, 'Mister Smythe, you are a most ungraceful dancer.'

'I don't often practice,' said Audrey, moving her feet as best she could in time with the strings. How, she wondered, was one meant to dance to music that had no drums to set the pace.

'Oh, don't you?' said Cordelia. 'I would not have thought you'd have any difficulty finding a partner.'

She spoke lightly, putting the barest hint of emphasis on *you*. Audrey chose her words carefully. 'Some gentlemen,' she said, 'I suppose might dance with any lady they take a fancy to – but I prefer to be more discerning.'

For a moment Cordelia looked right into her eyes. And that gaze, which Audrey held, was not flattered as much as frightened. There was heat there and what kind of heat it was she wasn't sure.

Cordelia turned her eyes away, placing her feet with utmost care. But when the music ended, she did not release Audrey's hand. She led Audrey away from the dancers, back to her table by the window. Her glove was silk and soft against Audrey's bare skin.

'Mister Smythe,' she said. 'You are a very charming gentleman.'

'Thank you,' said Audrey, knowing that half that statement was untrue and doubting the other half very much.

'I enjoy our conversations very much,' said Cordelia. 'But you ought to know I am promised to another man.'

Audrey's heart, much as she tried to still it, moved in her chest. 'You're engaged?' she blurted out.

'Not exactly,' said Cordelia. 'Papa has said nothing. But I am sure he has already made up his mind who I am to marry, and when.'

'Then,' said Audrey, 'may I dance with you again?'

What Cordelia might have said to that, she never knew. For with a clunk of solid heels upon polished boards Lord Montgomery stood beside them.

'Mister Smythe,' he said. 'I must congratulate you. It's been some time since any gentleman has been able to tempt my daughter to dance.'

While his tone was warm his eyes were wicked and when he smiled, he smiled showing all his teeth like an ape. Feeling suddenly very bare, Audrey released Cordelia's hand and at the same moment felt Cordelia release hers.

'He asked very nicely, Papa,' said Cordelia.

'I thought the lady looked lonely, my lord.' Audrey dipped a shallow bow to placate him.

'Lonely, eh?' The lord's hand slipped into the pocket of his embroidered coat and there it moved, shifting as if moving a coin between his fingers. It was a gesture that put Audrey in mind of the gamblers of the valleys of the capital, toying with their dice, with their takings, their lucky charms.

'Not lonely, Papa,' said Cordelia. 'And now, I think I am tired. Would you be cross with me if I went to lie down?'

'No, no, my dear, no.' Lord Montgomery squeezed her hand, and waved her away.

At the door, Cordelia looked back over her shoulder, and her eyes for a moment met Audrey's. Then she picked up her skirts, and was gone.

'Mister Smythe, you are quite the dancer,' said Lord Montgomery. 'For you have tired my daughter out with one dance.'

'I suppose I must be,' said Audrey with a forced laugh. She rested a hand upon his back and guided him towards the French windows. 'Might we take the air, my lord?'

'I suppose we might,' he said.

'Good show,' said Audrey.

She had meant to make tame conversation for a time, but as they stepped onto the veranda Lord Montgomery said, 'You aren't the first young man to be so taken with my daughter.'

'I don't doubt it.' Audrey gestured down the veranda. 'Shall we?'

'Quite.' Lord Montgomery walked stolidly ahead of her. 'You're a fine young gentleman, Mr Smythe,' he said, 'and you are welcome in my house. But pray stay away from my daughter. She has a delicate constitution. It won't do to overexcite her.'

'Of course, my lord.'

'And I hope you shall not be surprised or disappointed when I say that you would not be a good match,' said Lord Montgomery. 'A girl such as Cordelia needs a gentleman who is established – a man who is the master of his own household and who knows his way about the world. Someone to keep her safe, and secure.'

'I understand entirely, my lord.' Audrey remained a respectful pace behind him as she spoke. 'Be assured, I meant nothing by it.'

'I never doubted it,' said Lord Montgomery, which was surely a lie. He turned his gaze to the glittering stars overhead.

'If I may ask, my lord,' said Audrey. 'Is Cordelia betrothed?'

Lord Montgomery stopped, and turned to face her. They had passed now beyond the lights of the party and the path was steeped in shadows. 'Now, Mister Smythe, I shall tell you this in strict confidence,' he said. 'I have made a match. Pray do not tell Cordelia. It's best she hear it from me, and only when everything is in order, so that she not be unsettled.'

'Of course, of course,' said Audrey with a flippant wave of her hand. 'I wouldn't dream of telling her. Who is the match? If I may ask?'

'A great lord,' said Lord Montgomery. 'An old and dear friend of mine. He will take good care of her.'

'I understand,' said Audrey.

An old man, then. A man old enough to be her father. Cordelia would be passed from one bald, reeking old man to another like a horse sold at market.

'Now, let us take a turn about the summer house and then have another drink.' Lord Montgomery walked on. Audrey did not.

Uncurling her hand, she stepped into the meagre light of a curtained window and looked at what she held.

When Audrey had gone by the name of Tommy, one of her most lucrative trades had been that of the fingersmith. Her tiny hands had dipped into many a purse and a pocket, on the streets and in marketplaces where men and women were on their guards. Picking a man's pocket in his own garden? A trifle.

Not a coin; simply a brooch, a red and white cameo that bore upon it the image of a lady, her delicate features very like Cordelia's. There was no power in it that Audrey could sense, but turning it she could make out symbols upon the metal setting, not etched, but rather finely burned.

She closed her hand around the brooch and weighed up her options. She might crush it underfoot. She might simply throw it away, fling it into the darkness of the gardens – but it would be found. She could take it to the depths of the lake and there lose it altogether but he might notice it missing in scant moments, long before she could reach the edge of the gardens.

And who was to say he could not have another one made.

'My lord,' she said, raising her voice. 'I think you might perhaps have dropped this.'

'Hmm?' Lord Montgomery turned and she saw his hand go to his pocket.

He marched up the path and in the light his face was flushed. He snatched the brooch. 'Thank you,' he said tersely. 'Thank you very kindly.'

Audrey said, 'My pleasure.'

*

Above the fireplace in Cordelia's room there hung a portrait in the sweet pastels that had been in vogue some twenty years prior. 'Who's the lady?' said Audrey.

Cordelia barely glanced at the painting. 'My mother.' Seated at her dressing table, she began to comb her hair. Such an intimate thing to do, with a gentleman in the room. Audrey wondered for the first time if Cordelia might suspect.

'She's very lovely,' said Audrey.

'Papa says she was the second loveliest lady he ever knew,' said Cordelia.

Pacing Cordelia's room, looking at the white mouldings and the thick cloth of her curtains, Audrey said, 'Who was the loveliest?'

Cordelia looked at her with tired eyes. 'Me, of course.' She drew the comb through her hair once more and setting it down, began to pin her hair back for the night. 'If he knew you were here,' she said, 'he'd have you beaten, and me – well.' Looking into the mirror she said, 'What do you mean by coming here?'

She didn't fear Audrey. That much was apparent. 'I came to tell you that I'm leaving your father's house.'

'Oh.' Cordelia's hands stilled in the act of adjusting her hair. 'When are you leaving?'

'Tonight,' said Audrey. 'Now.'

Turning on her single-legged stool Cordelia said, 'You mean to slink away in the night, like a thief?'

'Very like a thief,' said Audrey. 'Come with me.'

Cordelia exhaled a deep, sad sigh the likes of which Audrey had rarely heard from one so young. 'I cannot.'

'You can,' said Audrey. 'My horse is outside. It's not hard.'

'I tell you, I *can't*,' said Cordelia. 'Or have you forgotten?' So saying, she drew back her skirts, revealing her glass ankle. The orange light of the fire danced within it. 'The moment Papa knows I am gone I'll be frozen.'

'He shan't notice till morning,' said Audrey. 'And look.' From her pocket she drew the brooch that bore the image of Cordelia's mother.

At the sight of it Cordelia made no sound, but she covered her mouth. 'You *are* a thief.'

Was she impressed, or merely appalled? 'A very nimble one,' said Audrey.

The key to his lordship's room hadn't been hard to steal. Before Audrey had been Mister Aubrey Smythe she had briefly been Ada and worked as a scullery maid. Below stairs in any house such as this there would be copies of all the keys.

And after a night of drinking of course the lord slept deeply, upon his back and snoring. He was not an imaginative man. The jewel box beside his head had been the obvious place and while the key was surely hidden on his person she had many talents, and a lock pick.

'It *is* this, isn't it?' Audrey held up the brooch to the light, pretty, hateful thing that it was. 'That he uses?'

'Yes,' said Cordelia. 'Though I can't imagine how he does it any more than I can imagine how you have it.'

'Take it. It should be yours.'

'Put it back where you found it.'

It wasn't that Audrey hadn't expected this – she had known it was possible that Cordelia might be so stubborn, or so afraid. It was only that she had had neither the time nor the inclination to plan for it. 'You could go, tonight,' she said. 'I could take you as far away from here as you please. You could be free of him. Tonight.'

'He's my father,' said Cordelia, 'and this is my home.'

'For how long?' said Audrey. 'You were right. He means to marry you, and to an old man.'

'You don't understand,' said Cordelia. 'You're a gentleman. You couldn't understand.'

'I'm not gentle,' said Audrey. 'And I'm not a man, Cordelia.'

Cordelia stared up at her, eyes narrowing in the semi-darkness, and Audrey braced herself. But Cordelia merely sighed, and said, 'I should have known you were too good to be true.'

'I'm sorry,' said Audrey, trying for once in her life to sound sincere. 'I never meant to deceive you – to deceive *you*.'

'Who are you really?' said Cordelia. 'What manner of creature are you?'

'My name is Audrey, and I'm whatever manner of creature I please. I've been a girl and I've been a boy. I've been a maid and a blacksmith's apprentice. I've been a prisoner and once I was almost a nun. And now I'm a gentleman. It's so much easier than people think.'

'What do you want from me?' said Cordelia.

'I only want to help you,' said Audrey. 'If you really don't want me to then I'll put it back in its box and we shall never speak of it again. If that's what you want.'

'It's not a matter of what I want.' Cordelia rose, stiffly, from her stool. 'That's what I learned, the day they took my legs. What I want is irrelevant.'

'It doesn't have to be.'

Walking away from her, Cordelia went to the window. She pulled back the heavy curtain and gazed out at the darkened garden. 'I thought, perhaps, you wanted to love me.'

'Cordelia.'

'So many men have wanted me,' said Cordelia. 'Since my first ball – I was only a girl. All the men desired me but none of them wanted to love me.' Letting the curtain fall closed she said, 'I suppose it was all a lie after all.'

'It wasn't a lie,' said Audrey.

Cordelia looked back at her over her shoulder, and her eyes were wet. 'Of course it was a lie.'

Audrey had loved, and wanted to love, any number of women, but only ever as Ada or Annie or Audrey. Not as Mister Aubrey Smythe. Never as Mister Smythe. It wouldn't be right, to deceive a woman that way. But with Cordelia it had been different.

'It wasn't a lie,' she said. 'I never lied to you – not about anything true. I do want to love you, even though you'll never have me.'

'You don't want to love me,' said Cordelia. 'Not the way a gentleman loves a lady.'

Audrey wanted to say, *Of course not, no, why would I ever want to love you like that?* She said, 'No – the way a woman loves a woman, when no one is watching.'

Stepping forward, feeling brave, she offered her hand.

She had not meant to admit this and she expected revulsion – horror, even – but Cordelia said only, 'Who are you really?'

Resigning herself, Audrey slid back into the diction of her birth, the diction of the streets and valleys of the capital. 'My name is Audrey Smith. My father was a drunk and my mother scrubbed floors for a living. I ran away when I was a little girl and I've been whoever I want ever since.'

The room was dark, the shadows long. The fire snapped. Cordelia took her hand. 'I haven't ridden,' she said. 'Not since.'

'You can ride with me,' said Audrey.

'I can,' said Cordelia. 'I can ride with you.' Squeezing Audrey's hand, she said, 'I shall need to change.'

*

In the night, Lord Montgomery's house with its lighted windows seemed to float above the plain. One hand holding Cordelia fast upon the horse, the other holding the reins, Audrey looked back at that hideous place.

'I dare say,' said Cordelia, 'you shan't be Mister Smythe any more.'

'I dare say,' said Audrey, 'you shan't be Lady Cordelia any more.'

'I dare say I shan't,' said Cordelia.

Behind them, the glittering lights of the house. Ahead of them the darkness, warm and smelling of the summer night. Audrey said, 'Shall we ride on?'

Cordelia said, 'I dare say we shall.'

# People Will Talk

by

Donna M Day

# People Will Talk

Amanda Barrett was unhappy. So, so unhappy.

She was sick of cruises through the galaxy, touring gas giants that all looked the same; she was tired of staring at identical-looking meteor rocks in Tiffany's and she'd had enough of being in this damn hotel. And most of all she was unhappy being Mrs Barrett, Dominic Barrett's wife. Dominic Barrett, humanitarian, environmentalist, all-round good guy and billionaire. Dominic Barrett perfect husband. Amanda Barrett luckiest woman in the galaxy. If only they knew.

She lay in bed blindly flicking through the streaming screen. Her face grinned at her from half of the content, dead eyes and veneered teeth. She heard the ensuite shower turn off and groaned. She rolled over and pushed her face into the pillows before he came back into the room, perfect white towel wrapped around his perfect tanned waist. It was funny how they still used towels. Showers hadn't contained water for about fifty years.

She heard him walking around. Dressing. He didn't speak to her. He never did. He didn't care for her so why would he? She heard him stop. She could feel his eyes on her, as he stood there coldly staring at her. She sighed into the pillows, knowing he would hear her, knowing he wouldn't really care. She rolled over and sat up, the sheet falling to expose her breasts. His hard stare remained fixed on her face.

'We have to go for breakfast now,' he said.

'I don't want anything,' she mumbled. 'I'm not hungry.'

'We don't want people to talk,' he stated, sounding like he couldn't care less either way. 'We have to go for breakfast now. People will talk.'

She massaged her right temple with her fingertips suddenly feeling very, very tired. 'Can't you do something!' she snapped at him. 'Do you have to just stand there staring at me? Can't you just read, or watch something, or just do something?'

He tilted his head, looking at her with perfect, uncomprehending eyes. 'Very well,' he said, walking over to one of the massive armchairs by the window with the view of Earth. He picked up her e-reader and stared at the screen. 'What would you like me to read?'

She groaned, burying her face under the bedding and wishing she'd known on her wedding day that this was how it would be.

It hadn't always been this way. When she'd first met Dominic he'd been enthusiastic and excited about everything, but especially her. His eyes had followed her around the site where they were rebuilding Paris. She'd fallen in love in what had been the most romantic city in the world. She hadn't known about the money then. That had been a surprise when he'd knelt down in the wasted street with his mother's engagement ring, the diamond the size of a fist.

After that had followed a whirlwind of cake testing, venue choosing, and ordering custom grown, real, actually grown flowers.

Then the serious talk with his parents. That moment when she was told about doing things for appearance's sake. We don't want people to talk. It would never do, people talking.

She'd been miserable ever since.

Amanda and Dominic had been prominently placed in the dining room by the hotel staff. Hotel Luna was obviously only frequented by the higher-ranking members of society but, still, having Earth's golden couple providing free advertising just by being there wouldn't hurt.

All waiting staff were androids now, but Hotel Luna had gone one step further and had their service staff fitted with wheels in place of feet so that they glided about quickly, ensuring everyone who wanted caviar, canapés and champagne had it immediately. Deano Garavito, the hotel's owner, revelled in the hideousness of human looking staff with clunky tyres at the end of their trouser legs. For him it was a symbol of human power. A declaration that no matter how lifelike droids became, *Homo sapiens* reigned supreme.

Mr Garavito slithered over to Dominic and Amanda's table. Dominic was smiling enthusiastically, he was able to when he put his mind to it. He was even managing the odd laugh. Garavito sat and told them of his plans for a covered garden so people could go outside for walks. Right now the hotel was an indoor affair only, as putting spacesuits on didn't quite click with the luxury travel people wanted.

Amanda noticed the waiters were beginning to bring the soup around. Thank God – she was starving after refusing to get out of bed this morning for breakfast. No one seemed to be talking. As she'd tried to explain to Dominic, they probably actually cared as little as he did.

The waiter stopped at their table with the huge tureen of hot tomato soup. Apparently, the tomatoes were even grown from seed. He spooned it into her bowl and then leaned towards Dominic's. He rapidly raised his hand and said, 'None for me thanks.'

'Very well sir,' the android replied and wheeled away. Amanda hadn't noticed her handbag strap sticking out from under the table.

The tureen had emptied over Dominic before she'd raised her spoon to her lips.

Garavito was up in a flash. 'You stupid idiot robot! Do you have any idea who that man is? You're made of metal! How the hell can you be so clumsy? Artificial intelligence! Artificial stupidity more like...'

He trailed off as he noticed Amanda leaning over her broken, smoking husband, trying to hide the skin melting off his cheek. Dominic had died in a building accident in New Paris before they were married. His parents had told her that they were having an android replica made. It had to be done. They couldn't let their fortune fall into the hands of the government so she still had to marry him and then she would inherit everything. She only had to keep up the pretence for three years at which point the estate would become legally hers and they could create another accident and mourn Dominic properly. All she had to do was smile, pretend everything was okay, and keep up appearances.

But now she was sitting on the floor of a restaurant, in a hotel on the moon, covered in soup, while the crowd stared at her as she tried to conceal the metal face of her cold, unloving husband.

People will talk.

# The White Wolf

by

Sarah Hindmarsh

# The White Wolf

I was fifteen the first time I saw the white wolf. She was with my uncle then, in the herder's cabin on the mountainside. She was a mere cub of six months old curled up on a blanket by the fire. She wasn't frightened of me, but she kept her distance. I tried to pet the fur between her ears, but she slid away, ghost-like, and my fingers never made contact with her coat.

'She's not tame for pettin' lad,' my uncle said. 'It'll not be long afore she leaves me completely.'

'Where'd you get 'er?' I asked.

'Found 'er in the woods, thought she'd be lucky if I looked afta 'er.'

'Is she?'

'You never heard abou' the white wolf lad?'

'No. They special or summat?'

'Very, they're meant to bring luck an' riches to anyone that looks afta them, an' bad luck to them that hunts 'em. Look at 'er eyes lad, look at the black. Normal wolf they'd be brown, but it's like she's got the whole night inside 'er eyes.'

There was certainly something compelling about her, although I don't know if I really believed she was lucky. She looked at me, and she knew me, in a way I don't think anyone had ever known me before, or since. I fancied I could see sparkles in her coat where no light was falling.

The wolf watched me go when I set off back to the village that afternoon. I felt calm, protected, as though not even the bears would have dared to touch me that day.

The next time I visited my uncle she was gone. The blanket by the fire was still there.

'In case she gets cold in the winter,' my uncle said when he caught me looking at it.

It was the middle of summer, but I understood.

I only saw the wolf once more while my uncle lived in his cabin. At least I think I saw her, I got a glimpse of midnight eyes peering out of the foliage and frosted fur flashing through the trees. Then she was gone. It always felt like someone, or something, was watching the cabin though. Watching over it.

The goats made so much money at the markets for the next few years that my uncle was able to buy a farm near the city. He left the cabin to me, along with a small sum of money. I had no goats, but I did have a young wife and an infant son, and we liked the mountains. We used the money to buy a few sheep and some furniture and raised our son, Tomak, in the wilderness, a simple, happy existence. We never moved the blanket from by the fire.

Tomak was twelve when she came back. I was chopping wood for the fire when she shuffled into the clearing. Her gait was stiff, her fur patchy and she looked hungry. At first I didn't believe it could be the same wolf. She should have died many years ago. Wolves rarely reached ten years old, let alone twenty. Then I looked into her eyes, and she looked back into mine, and I knew. It was her. I stood aside and she made her slow way across the clearing. Despite her advanced age and creaky joints she still moved with a hint of that same grace she had as a cub. She climbed the steps with some difficulty and headed straight to the blanket by the fire. She lay with eyes closed, an expression of sheer bliss on her face, in the same spot as the first time I had seen her all those years ago.

Tomak sat beside her and reached out a hand to touch her. My wife started forward but I held her back.

'Shh, just watch,' I said.

Tomak ran his hand over the fur on her head and shoulder. The places he touched seemed to shine afterwards. The wolf raised her head, but didn't curl her lip.

'How did she know to come here Da'?' Tomak said.

'She lived here as a cub, with Uncle Seb.'

'Wolves don' live that long Da'!'

'This one might be a bit special.'

The wolf looked at my son with those deep, knowing eyes, and something passed between them, an understanding. I realised she had known him for a long time. She had been watching us all these years, and it was Tomak that she had come home to. I'd always thought she would come back for me, but I wasn't the one she chose. She laid her head in Tomak's lap and he curled his fingers in the fur on the scruff of her neck.

'She don' have long left do she Da'?'

'No Son, I think she came home for one las' bit o' comfort afore she goes.'

Tomak sat all evening with the white wolf. He hummed a lullaby, one his mother had sung to him when he was a baby. The wolf slept, her feet twitching occasionally as she dreamt – of what I don't know, I like to think it was of deeper secrets than the haunts of rabbits in the mountains. My boy didn't move until the rise and fall of her chest stopped and her eyes stopped seeing. With tears in his eyes he looked up at me.

'We need to bury her proper Da',' he said.

'Of course.' It wouldn't even have crossed my mind to do anything else. 'We'll do it at first light in the mornin'.'

We left her resting by the fire that night, and buried her the next morning, before we even had breakfast. We dug the grave at the edge of the clearing, working in silence. Tomak did not complain about the work, even when the shovel wore blisters on his hands. Once it was done we stood with our heads bowed for a few minutes, shed tears of respect for the creature that had touched our lives so fleetingly but made such a deep impression.

I sent Tomak to collect kindling while I fed the animals. He had been gone barely two minutes when he came running back into the clearing, breathless with excitement.

'Da'! Da' look at this!'

He rushed to me, eyes bright, cradling something hidden in his jacket.

'Look what I found Da'!' he said, unzipping his jacket part way.

From between the folds of fabric appeared two coal black eyes framed by a pure white ruff. The eyes were barely open but already showed the same wisdom as the other white wolf.

'Can I keep 'im Da'? Can I?'

I reached my hand out to pet the cub and he burrowed his head under Tomak's arm. My fingers closed on empty air.

# Princess, Star, Brilliant

by

Rosie Garland

## **Princess, Star, Brilliant**

He names us for what is most precious: Pearl, Ruby, Amber, Jade; and I am Emerald. A man such as Papa does not toy with vulgar flower names: those tedious bouquets of Lilies, Roses and Jasmines that delight at bloom's instant, but rot right after the taking. As Papa has it, a flower sickens after it is cut, whereas a gem grows ever more valuable.

I am the youngest. I am also the prettiest, though I will deny it in public, for lies are becoming. They bring husbands of gold and steel, in whom a girl may set herself to her best advantage.

Five daughters, blessed with a father who has never once complained at the lack of sons, nor rejected our mother for her womb's imperfection. Though we are female, he treats us as prized objects. He has assured us that if he were to sever his agreement with Mama, we would not be cast out with her. Are we not the most enviable of creatures? We breathe relief; gather ourselves into the safe shelter of his hands, and all is well.

Our days are filled with private study, and Papa is the sweetest of teachers. From him we learn our quality, and how it may be raised with the touch of a meticulous man. Does a jewel not beautify by being turned over in the hand of an expert? Papa takes each sister in turn to demonstrate the truth of it. He permits us to observe how he handles us, girl after girl, so that we may learn the necessary procedures we shall undergo. We practice new words: connoisseur, sybarite, gratification.

*Shhh,* says Papa. *This is our secret.*

Secrets are the most delectable of morsels. We sisters share them, luscious as caramels hoarded from the Feast of the Three Kings, although that comes but once a year, and our tutelage in pleasure comes so many times it is impolite to keep count. A lady does not keep count. If she counts, she is not worthy of what is counted.

Papa may expend long moments on my sisters, but the longest, by far, are spent on me. I am his special girl, singled out for special schooling. He whispers, *you are the greatest of my achievements*. What daughter would not give anything to hear those words spoken by her Papa? I learn quickly at his knee. Drink each drop of masculine wisdom; fatten on knowledge he reserves for me. Oh Papa, sun of my life, who teaches me how to be the best of gems: to glint, to shimmer, to draw the eye of discerning men. I dream of the ways I shall be cut: heart, marquise, princess, star, brilliant.

In all families, there is an occlusion in the stone. Another daughter is birthed, and this time Mama has done too much insult and we do not see her again. But what a pet we make of little sister! Blessed with the name Diamond: radiant eyes, radiant face and incandescent happiness. I am not jealous. Not a bit of it, for Papa strokes my hair and tells me how Emerald is a rare creature, whereas Diamonds, for all the money that can be made, are found in great quantity. Papa always knows how to soothe me.

However, even gods make mistakes. If there were ever an error in Papa's judgement, it is to leave the cutting of this youngest gem too late. She grows up strange. Answers only to Di, even when I hazard it is a sure way to bring misfortune onto a girl's head. She wears her hair and body in a careless fashion and when I say she is like a boy, she roars laughter and asks *what is wrong with that?* I clap my hands to my ears, chide her for her noise and clatter.

I care for her, and wish her no harm, only for her to be less in love with ugliness. I try to instruct her about the many ways she can be made beautiful, tell her of princess, star, and brilliant.

'Half the stone is sacrificed when it's cut,' she scoffs. 'I'll stay rough, and keep every part intact.'

'And never shine?' I sneer, displaying the smirk Papa has complimented me upon.

'There are better things in life than glittering to please another.'

'It is better not to be, than be unworked.'

'Who spouts that rubbish?'

I confess this makes me angry, for they are Papa's words, and no one may slander Him. I will bear any manner of slight, but will countenance no one who offends Our Father, even if she is His blood. Which one may doubt, for why else did he put Mama aside, unless she made filth with a stranger? It is what women do, those with a flawed womb. I toss my head; call her a fool, how she should kneel in gratitude that I deign to pass my secret knowledge on to her. I tell her of Papa's special love, exceeding any love she can hope to win. I rant and rail at her refusal to learn, her wilful ignorance of all that is important.

When I am finished, I wipe my chin of spittle and compose my hands into a tidy arrangement. I wait for her to weep and beg forgiveness, this disobedient beast who presumes to make me feel small. But instead, she speaks quietly. Such words as I can never repeat, nor soil my tongue. She twists his gifts into vileness, his special secrets into sickness. She tells me I must escape, before it is too late. I do not understand such madness, nor do I wish to.

Next morning there is a rope of knotted sheets hung from her window, a crushed rosebush at its foot. I pretend grief at the appointed times, when sorrow may be shown to its best advantage. Perhaps she is with Mama and all the other useless, unruly women. If it were not a misfortune of their own making

I might feel pity for them: the imprecision of their flesh; how their bodies spread like mongrel weeds; their lives of hideous work; the way they drag down the delicate reputation of our sex; that they have only each other, whereas I have everything a girl can dream of.

There is value in scarcity. We are five again and need no more sisters. Without her distraction, I shine brighter. I do not miss her. Yet, at night, her words hover around my head and whine like mosquitoes. One day, I will crush them and all memory of her. See, I have almost snuffed out her name.

One by one, my elder sisters go, to be set in fine marriages. I grow, and as my body blooms I rejoice in each of Papa's lessons. His hands, precise and steady as a cutter of gems. I strive to become perfect. I gleam. I glitter. He displays me, often. I turn slowly, to show off each pretty part. There are crowds of eyes upon every gleaming piece of me. Their gaze increases my beauty, and beauty is my value. What a price I will fetch! How I will crow when all is signed and done and I am given over to be hammered, clamped, burnished and secured in claws. Look deep, and in me you will not find the tiniest fault. I am princess, star, brilliant.

# Fossils

by

Becky Cherriman

## Fossils

This boy, Tom, is lifting a stone from the riverbed. He peers closer, deciphers the greyed wings of a prehistoric fly, traces a shell in relief. A few metres away, two girls splash one another in the shallow water, uninterested by fossils, at least for now. Hania and Fern are at the tipping point between childhood and adolescence. Nubs have begun to swell on their chests, fine hairs curl under their skirts. They have stopped pulling faces when they pass mirrors. Instead they look more frequently and for longer.

This is the game – to keep the face as static as possible. The expression should be blank, all traces of a smile removed. Or, if there is a smile, it must be carefully prepared. If quick enough, the expression will have been crafted before it's reflected back. If quick enough, the symmetry demanded by the screens – those signifiers of beauty – will be attained. If nobody is looking, the game can continue for up to an hour. If they can only discover the cause of their asymmetry, they will be able to determine what can correct it. Too clumsy looking. Too shy. Not stylish enough. The mirror belies their failures; it dissects them. Lower right cheek. Pimpled right nostril. The more they become victims of their own gaze, the more pieces they find themselves in.

Tom, although he is the same age and so a little behind the girls in terms of physical changes, plays the game too. At the tipping point, faults emerge which had previously gone unobserved. His nose squashes to one side. The mild squint is so exaggerated he might be looking in all directions at once. In certain lights his skin appears leathery; he imagines this is the sign of a new superpower, that he is half boy, half reptile. He is still young enough to fantasise about superpowers: old enough to see the monstrous in himself.

None of them has ever won the game.

At big social occasions the boy hides himself under a hood while the girls cover their faces with their hands, their feelings under giggles. But the three of them, raised side-by-side as neighbours, have not entirely grown out of the habit of being children together so disappointment in their bodies is temporarily banished when they are together.

Barefoot, ignoring the asymmetrical selves flickering back at them from the water, the girls step from rock-to-rock while Tom remains absorbed in the fossil, toes numb against the current. They are an inch away from a sharp dip in the riverbed, by the path through the wood that runs beside it, at the moment when everything will change.

Then – a noise. An almighty crack that splinters everything – bark, air, youth itself.

They might, if they had chance to think, believe it to be thunder because of the great wind and rustling that accompanies it. But the sky is a fairy tale blue that does not permit the possibility of storms. It is not thunder.

Until this moment they have heeded the advice of their mothers and have stuck to the permitted route, at most venturing only a step or two away. Now instinct kicks in. They run, eardrums trembling with aftershocks, waves of air slapping at their cheeks. They reach for one another's hands, unsure if the direction they are going is the right one but knowing if they don't leave the path something horrific will happen.

Gunshot and its echo, thinks the boy. A drug dealer from the estate seeking revenge for an unpaid debt, thinks Hania. A hunter out to claim the skin of a great animal, thinks Fern.

Their feet slow on beechnuts and old twigs. They turn.

'Just a tree,' Fern says. A newly felled oak, skirted by leaves, crushed and torn.

'A tree,' Hania agrees.

Tom starts to laugh, setting all of them off, expanding their joy till it liberates them from one another's grasp, leaving them breathless.

They move closer to the oak, touch it tentatively as though it is a giant they are fearful of awakening. Growing in confidence, Fern tests a branch before swinging up onto it. Hania joins her. On the pads of their hands and knees, they clamber across the breadth of three bigger branches, their odd horizontal climb making it seem like the laws of space have been torn up with the roots of the tree.

Tom squints, disorientated. He asks them to come down, suggests circumnavigating the oak to find their way home. He actually says 'circumnavigate', a word he heard once on a documentary about Jules Verne. He likes it because it is a word you can really get your lips around and because it makes him sound more grown up, less scared of climbing trees, or of not being able to find the way home.

They cannot go around the tree because the foliage surrounding it is so dense; every time they try to break through branches whip them back, leaving marks on their faces and legs. In blocking their path, the tree has also blocked their past because there is no other way but away from home, to somewhere they haven't ventured before.

'Did you hear the noise it made? Crack. Kaboom.' Hania leaps up in the air and gestures with her arms.

'I thought it was a bomb.'

'An earthquake.'

'Gunshot.'

Creaking.

They look around, wary. To their right – a shrivelled sapling, bent by its early death, wavers in the wind.

The wood has forgotten the heat of the day. The foliage

thickens, making a Chartreuse treacle of the air. Soil and spores clog the back of their throats, slowing their talk. Hania notices her dress is slipping down one shoulder. She straightens it, embarrassed. Tom puts up his hood. They proceed – sullen, estranged from one another, from their child selves, until...

...a large glade dashed with stones, the far end demarcated by the edge of a huge rock. They hasten towards it, find carved into the stone a set of steps. They gasp. The steps remind them of a recurring dream. It is a dream they share although its form shifts and warps each time it is dreamed.

Each of them, alone, jumps from the top of a set, no, it must be a flight of stairs for, on leaping, they find themselves flying. This behaviour is forbidden and it is intensely pleasurable. In some manifestations of the dream, the stairs are carpeted in beige or an Indian-patterned red and gold. In others they are back door steps – iron and coated in a black peeling paint, descending, perhaps, from the room above a shop.

These stairs before them, however, are stone and the three children find themselves not at the top but at the bottom. They wind upwards into a huge castle, its discoloured turrets just visible above the treetops.

A castle.

There is no moment so terrifying, so wonderful as the moment you realise the woods you have known all your lives are not what you believed them to be.

They have never been this far into the thicket but they know there was no castle here this morning or yesterday or last year or ever in any of the stories their parents told them. Except... wasn't there a bedtime tale Fern's mother span as Fern clutched her hot chocolate in a room of wooden hearts and porcelain bears? A tale of a castle with turrets like those we all once built atop bricks of alternating colours? A castle shaped much like this one, which appears to be hewn out of the natural stone. A castle with a staircase. What was it her mother said about the staircase?

Despite his tendency to cautiousness, Tom takes the lead. Perhaps he has already begun to internalise expectations of masculinity, believes he must be the one to confront the danger, the one to defeat it. Or is it rather the thrill of the dream that somersaults him into the part of alpha male, his greed for the treasure at the top?

Whatever the reason, Hania and Fern ascend after him. Their minds cling to memories before shedding them, step-by-step:

Cloud swirl above the roundabout.

Bobbing in a wave pool with a younger sibling.

Small hands turning a supermarket item on the self-checkout before passing it to Mum.

The grip of a football boot on mud.

Fingers reddening around the handle of a book bag.

A scent harvested from rose petals on the turn.

These are the thoughts of the three, moments that have, of late, been replaced by hair straighteners, the right trainers and all the newly discovered imperfections of their bodies. These too are paraphernalia falling from them as they rise.

A resonance courses between the stone steps and their bodies, elicits from them a deep yearning. They have no name for the feeling or awareness of the object it seeks to attach to but the feeling is so strong it overwhelms all that has gone before. Halfway up the stairwell, they no longer know where they came from.

Finally they emerge into a great hall.

'Is there anyone there?' Tom asks.

Nobody answers.

The table is laid out for a huge feast – venison, a boar's head, carrots, swedes, cabbages, a plate of nuts. Hania's gaze settles on the tarnished silver cutlery. She was hungry, she remembers.

This time it is Fern, body still humming with the song of the stairs, who steps forward first into the odour of stale hops.

Closing in, they find everything is rotting. Maggots undulate across the tablecloth. The carrots are shrivelled and diseased. Flies eat out the eyes of the boar.

'Who was here?'

'What happened to them?'

Why have they left the ruined feast splayed out to torment us? Hania cannot bear to look at the waste.

She rushes past it towards a stone passage at the end of the hall, steps out into a room plush with velvet and mahogany furniture and a frieze cut into the stone wall. In the centre – an enormous four poster bed with a stone fireplace at its foot. Above that – an ostentatious gold mirror. She approaches.

Forgetting the others, she looks at her lips – plush, blood-flushed. The line of her cheekbones. The sweep of her brows. Her eyes amber not just in colour but in the complexity of forms that make them up. This is her – Hania – perfect enough to be a celebrity, an actress on a make-up ad. Symmetrical. Beautiful. She cannot rip her gaze away.

Fern joins her at the mirror and Tom too but she doesn't register them. Nor do they notice her; so intent are they on finding the symmetry that until now has eluded them, they grow lost in the sublime landscapes of themselves.

As the afternoon closes in, shadows creep over them, unseen.

Afterwards Hania will say she doesn't know what it was that made her remember the hunger but there must have been something in the quality of it that was stronger even than the spell wrought by the mirror. Something so powerful it pulls at her, makes her see their gaze and all else of them captured in the glass.

She has not seen her friends as she perceives them in this mirror. Tom's dark run of hair over his forehead, his cheekbones, the swell of biceps under his T-shirt. Fern's eyes and the flawless sweep of her brows. Hania cannot stop looking at her collarbone, the swell of her breasts underneath. Perfect. And yet, and yet... the essence of the friends she knows is gone, all the edges of them rubbed off. Inanimate, they are two-dimensional, a series of marks that don't make up anything recognisable as a whole. And behind them on the wall by the bed – the stone frieze made up of... life-size figures.

She snaps her eyes shut, steps back from the mirror, turns to the frieze. Two of the figures are oddly clothed in what look like jeans and T-shirts. They hold heroic poses: his – fist pressed to chest, eyes raised: her's – arms outstretched as though mid-charge. As Hania stares at the wall, she notices other figures in varying states and styles of dress.

She glances back at her friends. Understands. Turns first to Tom and then to Fern. But no, they are still transfixed. She doesn't blame them because, oh, they are beautiful but... No. She wrenches herself away, tears the thick eiderdown from the bed, reaches underneath for the sheets, flings one over Tom, the other over Fern. Spins them both away from the glass.

She calls their names – gentle – and they stir as though the sheets are pupal skins and they're awakening to metamorphosis. She thinks of the book she saw about moths, how they edge out as though still believing themselves caterpillars. Head first, antennae next, they cling to their cauls. Not yet aware they have wings, they swing, get their balance and then...

She plucks the shrouds from them. 'Look.'

'What are you doing?' Tom says, irritable as though disturbed from a not-long-enough sleep. His eyes are an entranced milky green.

The wall is crammed with figures from different eras – dozens of them. Between the figures are spaces for more. Hania doesn't take her gaze from Tom's face – his real face, not the reflected one. She steps back till she's pressed up against the frieze.

Tom's eyes clear. He blinks. Blinks again. It is as though the space was made for Hania. He envisions her dress fading, her features turning grey.

Fern recognises it too. She reaches out for her hand, tugs her out of harm's reach.

'You see,' Hania says, 'We have to go.'

Tom traces the outlines of the figures with his hand, pauses on the stone spaces the three of them could have filled. They exchange a long, grown-up look and run. They dash along the corridor, past the hall with its uneaten feast and descend the stairs, collecting their memories as they go.

Under the watchful eyes of the wood, Tom halts. 'That mirror...'

'We would have been perfect,' Fern breathes.

'Trapped,' says Hania.

'Fossils,' says Tom.

Cramped up close to one another, surrounded by trees, they wonder – can this really be Tom with his spots and Adam's apple? Is this Fern with growing breasts? Hania, who has a faintly sweet and adult aroma? What is it they still do not know of one another? Caterpillar, chrysalis, moth.

Hunger tugs between them. They smile then, comprehending the dream; from one another's bodies they will learn that there are other ways home.

# Human Point-oh

by

Jonty Levine

# Human Point-oh

Everyone was saying the Update would be the best thing to happen to humanity since opposable thumbs, or some other huge milestone. It was going to carry us to a new plane of existence. Or possibly destroy us, we just didn't know. I personally didn't buy all the hype – 'It's just a *point-one* update,' I'd say when someone brought up the topic.

Don't get me wrong – it *was* a big deal. I can see why the news channels were covering it 24/7, despite there being nothing new to cover. Of course people took to the internet to speculate. And I saw an interesting essay about how a benevolent god might have planned the update to remove all prejudice from our minds. But most every other comment seemed to be someone's personal wish-list of awesome superpowers.

And yes, it *was* all of us. 7 billion people saw the progress bar at the exact same time, in the corners of their eyes, at 1% and counting. Alongside it were a few words telling them they would soon be updated to Version 1.1 of humanity. No one yet knew what this would do to us, or if there was any way to stop it. Some people actually committed suicide before it finished, reasoning that if they were to be changed into something that wasn't human, they'd rather die with their humanity intact.

So yes, I could see why this was a big deal. It's just... I wish it wasn't.

After three months, the progress bar reached 100%, and something happened that I didn't expect. No one was changed immediately, but in the corners of our eyes there appeared a new notification: *Human Update 1.1. Hold your breath for 10 seconds to finish installation.*

It was so simple, don't breathe for a moment and that was it. Most people were afraid to try it, and rightly so. But with 7 billion of us all poised to undergo the same transformation, someone was bound to go first. People curious to see what would happen, and those with nothing to lose, were among the early adopters. Within the first eleven seconds of it being offered to them, they were bathed in a silvery light, and then...

Luckily for them, the effects were *non*-deadly. Those who'd been counting on a biblical apocalypse were duly disappointed. In fact, the most immediately obvious change was the loss of all freckles as they gained a marble-smooth complexion. Over the next few hours, those who underwent the change lost all unnecessary hair, except for that on top of their heads. Conversely, bald people's hair grew back. And hair that'd gone grey with age regained its colour. People frequently compared it to the various interface improvements and bug fixes of a typical software update. Losing their freckles, I suppose, was one of these "improvements".

Over the next few weeks, some of the subtler changes in the upgraded humans became apparent. Their vulnerability to certain autoimmune diseases went away, while the pharmaceuticals became more expensive for the rest of us. Poison ivy ceased to have an effect on them. And allergies to nuts went away entirely. One of the more interesting changes though was the reduced need for sleep. People who'd undergone the update, or "human point-ones", found they felt fully rested after 3 or 4 hours sleep, as opposed to the usual 7 or 8 hours for us "point-ohs".

And yes, I am still a point-oh. We still exist, thank you very much. I don't need a reason for not "upgrading", though I do have one. I like the freckles, okay? I also think some men look better with beards – there I said it! I don't want to change just because everyone else is. I think the update robs us of our differences. It's well known that some subtle racial features are erased by the update, but none of the point-ones seem to care.

And those people are now the vast majority. Within the first week, over 60% of the world population had changed into point-ones, and people like me are in an ever-dwindling minority.

It's getting harder and harder to live normally without finishing the installation, becoming like one of them. They won't let us rest! Since we're supposed to all sleep for four hours a night, we're now expected to spend the extra time working. Because heaven forbid anyone should actually enjoy four extra hours a day!

There is this widely held belief that the update really did erase our prejudices. Most of this however is pure media spin. While it is true that racism is going out of fashion, and some old grudges have been set aside, the truth is that point-ones *are* more tolerant... towards each other. Yet they see nothing wrong with treating the point-ohs as an inferior species. 'If you don't like it, accept the update,' they always say.

That's not the only benefit, they say. It also increases your self-control towards food. It will improve your sex life, they say. Those point-ones all think they're so bloody perfect! And don't think I haven't considered taking the update on my own terms. All I'd have to do is hold my breath for 10 seconds. But that's the scary part. If I'm not careful, I could do it accidentally. Anyway, it's become a matter of principle now. Having to wait for hiccups to go away on their own is the least of my problems.

Remaining a point-oh has had its challenges, but I wouldn't have it any other way. If I can avoid this update for as long as possible, preferably the rest of my life, then it might have been worth something. And after I'm gone, I hope they put me in a museum, so that future generations might be able to gaze upon my grey hair and imperfect skin, and learn of a strange extinct species that once ruled the world: human point-oh.

# The Fox's Wedding

by

Carys Crossen

## The Fox's Wedding

Some villages have a Village Beauty, but this particular village had a Village Ugly.

It was agreed by most of the villagers that Morwen, the innkeeper's daughter, was by far the ugliest woman for miles around. She was tall, standing just an inch shy of six feet, with long black hair she scraped back in a bun. She had a hooked nose, a square jaw and the eyes of a hangman. When Morwen turned her dark gaze on a man, she always gave the impression that she was calculating how far he'd drop from the gallows; whether his neck would snap or if the noose would throttle the life out of him.

In truth, Morwen was no more ill-favoured than most girls in her village. Some might secretly have found her strong features and raven-wing hair quite striking. But Morwen had two characteristics that worked against her.

One was her savage honesty. It did not matter if you were the squire's wife or the mayor, or the drunk who slept in the manure pile of the stables for warmth. Morwen would tell you exactly what she thought of you and your actions. This was not a pleasant experience for most of the villagers. We all indulge in fantasies about ourselves and our abilities and our social standing on occasion, or even all the time, and her brutal brushing aside of such illusions had reduced more than one unfortunate wretch to tears, or drink, or both.

Morwen's frankness stemmed from her other disconcerting trait, which was that she knew things. Most people know a few things, or pretend to, but Morwen's knowledge was uncanny, for she knew things nobody else did. She knew what the weather would do on the morrow, whether it would rain or blow or stay dry. She knew which of the sheep on the hillside would have twin lambs. When Widow Jenkins lost her wedding ring, it was Morwen who told her where to find it – in a rip in the sheet covering her feather bed, nestled in amongst the goosedown.

'She's mad, a harridan, a scold. She's ugly as an ape,' people muttered, always out of Morwen's hearing. For Morwen's knowing extended to *them*. She knew when the wife of the magistrate had spent the night in the baker's bed. She knew the squire's fair daughter Marigold had fallen in love with the strong, handsome blacksmith, and was pining in secret as her father arranged a marriage with some chinless baronet's son. (And she knew Jonty the smith loved Marigold too but had been sent packing by her father.) She knew the wool-merchant was bored with his long-suffering wife and was looking up pretexts for an annulment.

To wit, Morwen was a most uncomfortable neighbour, and the villagers revenged themselves by insulting her looks, which most girls would have found unbearable. But Morwen cared little for other folks' judgements. The glass told her she was no great beauty, but nor was she hideous as people made out. And so she continued helping her father and mother run the inn, always waiting and hoping for something to happen.

What that something was, Morwen could not have told exactly. But she knew she possessed a cooler head and quicker wits than most, she knew a great many things that others didn't, and she knew she was destined for more than making beds and serving ale in a provincial village where the greatest excitement was when the mayor's pig-headed pig got loose and ate someone's turnips.

And so she swept and scrubbed and carried pints of ale as customers called for them, and bartered at market and continued to upset their neighbours. It was fortunate that her family's alehouse was the only one for twenty miles roundabouts, surrounded by wind-scrubbed moors, or trade might have suffered. But life went on as it always had done and looked set to do for fifty years and more.

Then one day a stranger came to the village.

Strangers did sometimes pass through the village, but they were weary travellers, dusted with the dirt of the journey. Or they were travelling merchants on their way to trade at a port or great city, or they were peddlers, or soldiers on their way to re-join their regiments. This stranger was none of these things, and so was very strange indeed.

He was a handsome man, well-dressed in a fancy velvet frock coat and a lace cravat. He carried a silver-topped cane, his movements were swift and decisive, his dark eyes darted from side to side unceasingly and his teeth were creamy and sharp. He strolled down the main street, smiling to himself as though it pleased and amused him to behold the little village and the simple, straightforward villagers it contained.

The village girls looked askance at him, and giggled and blushed and whispered behind their hands. The village lads rolled their eyes and grumbled, knowing no lass would bother flirting with them when a greater prize was up for grabs. Mothers eyed the stranger, torn between the prospects and dangers a wealthy stranger represented for pretty, marriageable village maidens.

And Morwen, polishing pewter behind the bar, felt a cold sweat break out across her forehead, as though Death's hand had brushed her face and left its shallow imprint there.

She set down the tankard she'd been buffing and darted outside. The handsome newcomer was seated beside the town fountain, a small crowd of sycophants already gathered about him.

Morwen looked at him, and she knew. She knew that the man by the fountain was no man at all, but something wild and beastly and dark.

And the man who was no man felt Morwen's gaze upon him, and though his eyes never once strayed in her direction, his grip upon his cane tightened until his knuckles turned pale and bloodless.

\*

Reynardine, his name was. Squire Reynardine, the last scion of a wealthy family from the South, come on a walking holiday to this lonely, remote region. A few villagers, Morwen among them, raised their eyebrows when it was revealed he travelled without servants or luggage, but the great golden pieces he proffered were enough to assuage the curiosity of most. The mayor offered him a room in his townhouse, as the inn was clearly beneath such a grand gentleman and Reynardine accepted graciously.

A short time later, the local notary, a man with three daughters still unwed, went to visit with the mayor on business he'd been happily putting off for weeks. By the time he left he had wrangled an invitation to dinner at the mayor's house that night.

That same evening, in the inn, as men and women laughed and gossiped and speculated about the mysterious stranger, Morwen glided outside into the dark night, as soft and silent as a shadow on snow.

She made her way through the alleyways and yards and bits of overgrown scrub, keeping out of sight of anyone peering through their window or out doing some mischief. Morwen moved as swiftly and as sure-footedly as a vixen, for she had played throughout the village since she was a toddling babe and knew its every cobblestone.

She came to the mayor's house, stepped up on a crate the servants had left outside and peered in at the window. Squire

Reynardine was supping there, eyes bright and hungry as he chatted with the notary's prettiest daughter, Evangeline. The girl was giggling at something he was saying, her flushed face and unthinking smile a testament to her infatuation.

Morwen stepped down from the crate, and scrabbled about on the ground until her hand closed on a stone, picked out of a horse's shoe that afternoon by a careful ostler. She drew her arm back past her head in an unladylike fashion, and let it soar.

The window pane splintered, the glass clattering down to rest on the windowsill and the carpet of the dining room. Shouts and shrieks escaped into the night, and the dinner party descended into chaos. Morwen slipped away, and was back serving ale in the inn before anyone had collected sufficient wit to notice she had been gone for a while.

\*

Squire Reynardine left town the next day. His road took him past the inn, and his pace as he passed it was dangerously close to a gallop.

Very early the day after Squire Reynardine departed, before even the scullery maid was up, Evangeline left her family's house and made for the road that led up the bleak and barren moors.

As the sun passed the high point of the sky, and began to lower itself towards the horizon, it occupied one half of the sky. In the other half, clouds made dark with rain and ill-feeling gathered and soon the rain pelted down.

Morwen looked up at the sky, half sunlit and half sunk in shadow, and she shivered. A fox's wedding, the local farmers called it, when there was both rain and sun in the sky.

\*

By nightfall the whole village knew Evangeline was missing. Villagers lit lanterns and bravely wandered the hills and roads roundabouts, calling for her, searching for her.

Morwen was not among them. She knew Evangeline would never be found.

*

They didn't find Evangeline, not a hair on her head or a button off a boot. People surmised she had eloped with a lover and would return married and triumphant or unmarried and pregnant. But neither happened, and eventually, the hubbub died down and people went about their business, kindly averting their gazes from the reddened eyes of the notary and his remaining family.

Two months passed. And then Squire Reynardine returned.

As soon as he set foot in the village Morwen knew. She abandoned the dinner she was cooking and fled outside, but she was too late. Already the rector was bowing low to him, gesturing towards his house. And Squire Reynardine was walking along with the rector, who was quite willing to walk with the new arrival.

Morwen scowled so fiercely that the butcher, walking along towards her, crossed the street to avoid a confrontation. For the rector had a pretty young daughter, who despite her pious upbringing was a coquette who revelled in masculine attention.

By that afternoon Reynardine was out walking with the girl, who was called Rosamund. She was casting her most alluring looks at him, smiling coyly, fluttering her eyelashes, arching her back so as to show off her figure.

Morwen stepped into their path. Reynardine halted as though he'd run his handsome nose into a brick wall and his small dark eyes glittered with spite.

'What did you do to Evangeline?' Morwen demanded, her voice loud enough to be heard by half the village.

'I'm sure I don't know what you mean, *hag*,' Reynardine said with a smirk. Rosamund tittered.

Morwen whipped out the knife she used for jointing chickens and held it under Reynardine's chin. His smirk vanished and he snarled, lips lifting from long teeth. His thin nose twitched. Rosamund screamed and sank into a graceful swoon.

'Leave,' Morwen spat. 'Or I'll tear you apart. You won't be the first fox I've skinned.'

Reynardine's face turned white as salt at those words. But before Morwen could carry out her threat, the villagers were upon them, dragging Morwen away, snatching at the knife as she struggled and fought like a trapped bear.

Reynardine scooped the swooning Rosamund into his arms and watched with vengeful satisfaction as the villagers dragged Morwen to the town hall's cellar, to be locked in until her temper cooled. It took a long time. She was banging at the walls and yelling like a wild thing all afternoon and well into the night, and even the strongest men dared not enter, not even to take her some food.

Reynardine, discomposed by what was obviously the local madwoman (or so he said to the rector) decided to take his leave. He left, his ears ringing with apologies, while people shook their heads at Morwen's actions. The girl had always been a virago, a bit peculiar, but this was beyond the pale. Clearly her ugliness and lack of marriage prospects had sent her doolally. Her poor, mortified parents shut up the inn early that evening, unable to bear the gossiping and scolding of their neighbours.

*

Late that night, long after her prayers were supposed to be said and she was supposed to be tucked up asleep, Rosamund left the parsonage by means of the servant's door and headed off for a moonlit walk on the moors. She giggled as she walked, for of course she wasn't going to walk alone. Where was the pleasure in that? No, Rosamund was going to meet a man, and there would be flirting and kissing and maybe even a present or two off such a rich gentleman as she was going to meet.

As Rosamund walked up the path to the moors, bleached bone white in the moonlight, she observed that across the moor, the rain was falling from dark clouds that veiled the stars. But her way was dry, and brightly lit. She walked on.

And in the cellar, Morwen finally fell silent. Too late now.

\*

Rosamund's disappearance was known throughout the village before the sun had crept all the way above the horizon. Her vanishing cast a very different light on Morwen's violent behaviour. One pretty girl going missing after a visit from a mysterious stranger could have been coincidence, but two was most irregular. The chastened villagers ran to let Morwen out as soon as it became evident that Rosamund was gone, and the rector even humbled himself to ask for her help.

But she only shook her head at him.

A search was carried out, of course it was, but Rosamund could not be found. And despite his looks and his wealth, Squire Reynardine could no longer be considered above suspicion. The villagers even began muttering that they should have let Morwen slit his throat, for didn't the girl know things than no one else could know?

Hindsight is a wonderful moral compass. People always do the right thing in hindsight.

The only man who dismissed the talk of Squire Reynardine's guilt was the village's Squire, whose family name was Mallinder. Squire Mallinder was adamant no gentleman (such as himself) could be responsible for such unchivalrous behaviour towards young ladies. Why, he had spoken with Squire Reynardine himself and the man was most agreeable! Those poor missing girls had run afoul of some highwayman on the road or fallen into a ravine. Was such a gentleman to be slandered because some plain, insignificant village wench had cast the finger of suspicion upon him?

But the villagers, who had never had a great opinion of their squire, continued to mutter uneasily about Reynardine and his pointed teeth and his rat-shrewd eyes.

\*

Reynardine might have been wicked, but he was not a complete fool. He did not return to the village for months. But he was just a *little* foolish, and so return he did. Besides, he had the outlaw's love of defying the odds, and he found the chance to thwart such a determined adversary as the unsightly Morwen irresistible.

When he returned, he scrupulously avoided the inn and the townsfolk and went straight to call on Squire Mallinder in the big house on the hill. His welcome off the squire and his family was most warm and gracious (save for Miss Marigold, who was pining for her blacksmith). But the servants were wiser, and within minutes of Reynardine's arrival a maid left her dusting and slipped down to the inn to fetch Morwen.

Morwen asked the maid to stay at the inn to help her mother and father, and ran pell-mell to the big house on the hill. She tapped at the kitchen door, and the cook let her in without a word of protest.

Morwen borrowed an apron from another maid and all afternoon she went about housework, keeping out of sight as a good servant ought. But Morwen had the ears of an owl, and no scruples whatsoever about listening at keyholes. In a very short time she learned that Marigold's marriage to the baronet's son was no longer in the realms of possibility. But Squire Mallinder thought such a gallant gentleman as Squire Reynardine would be glad to be better acquainted with his lovely daughter Marigold.

Morwen tore off her apron and ran to the kitchen.

'Tell Marigold I'll be outside her window tonight at ten o'clock, and under no circumstances is she to go walking alone with Reynardine,' she whispered to the cook, who promised faithfully to deliver the message.

And away Morwen went, back to the inn. She had plans to make.

\*

Alone in her room after dinner, Marigold waited in a frenzy. She got quite a shock when there was a tap at her window, and she opened it to find Morwen clinging like a squirrel to the ivy that shrouded the house.

'Has he asked you to walk with him?' Morwen asked at once, manners be damned.

'Yes!' Marigold answered. 'And Papa's insisting I go. But I don't want to!'

'You won't,' Morwen said coolly. 'Tomorrow morning, tell your father you want to walk to town to buy some marzipan for Squire Reynardine before you walk with him. Wear your longest cloak, and make sure you go alone. When you get there, come to the inn. I'll be waiting.'

She said nothing more, but Marigold was a bright enough

girl. She risked squeezing Morwen's hand in gratitude, and then watched as Morwen climbed nimbly down the ivy and vanished into the gloaming.

\*

Morning came early, as usual. Despite the drizzle that threatened to become a deluge, Marigold came to the inn as promised, explaining that she'd arranged to meet Reynardine up on the moors. To her delight, Jonty the smith was waiting with Morwen, two of his heaviest hammers clutched in his formidable fists.

'Jonty's here to defend the inn if anything goes awry,' Morwen explained briefly. 'Here, quick, give me your cloak.'

Marigold did so, and Morwen put it on. Without a word she made for the door.

'Best of luck, Morwen,' said Jonty.

'And thank you!' said Marigold.

Morwen paused, nodded to them, and left.

\*

It showered steadily as Morwen hiked up to the moor, shortening her usual stride so she walked sedately, as a proper lady ought to. It hadn't escaped her notice that it was only raining in one half of the sky. The other half was as fair as you could wish.

Morwen smiled grimly as she minced along. Tucked under her cloak she carried a sharp knife, a mirror and her apron, rolled up loosely.

She caught sight of Reynardine well before he spotted her. He was waiting near the only shelter for miles around: a rocky outcropping that rose above the rough grasses and heather, and provided a windbreak. Morwen moved as quickly and quietly as she could, but before she had taken three steps he turned and espied her.

He raised a hand in greeting as Morwen hurried towards him. She had pulled the hood of Marigold's cloak down low over her face, but she peered from underneath it and saw his face split into a wide smile, that stretched from ear to ear. She shuddered. It was as though his face had been slashed wide open and the wound was gaping, running red.

'Hello, my beauty!' he called. 'A miserable day for a walk, but no matter. We can shelter here until the rain passes.'

Morwen walked up to him, keeping her eyes on the ground.

'Why so coy, my lovely?' Reynardine crooned, raising a hand. He made to pull back her hood, but Morwen was too quick for him. She whipped out her mirror and held it up to his face.

And then – and then. Reynardine took one look in that mirror and howled. No human throat could have produced that keening, that high wild shrilling. And then, and even Morwen shuddered to see it, and then his skin began to melt, peeling and falling away from his bones. No, not his bones – for there was fur underneath that handsome face, and a long pointy nose, and sharp white teeth, and claws at the end of his fingertips...

Not man, nor fox, but some strange monstrous melding of both. The worst of man and the worst of beast. The mirror showed Reynardine for what he truly was. He glared at Morwen with hatred blazing red in his eyes, and he lunged for her, claws outstretched to tear out her throat.

Morwen broke the mirror swinging it against his face, and the glass fell to rest unheeded in the turf. Reynardine retreated, monstrous face bleeding, and Morwen drew her knife. They circled each other, two wild creatures, both knowing that the end was near for one of them.

Then Reynardine's inhuman lips curled back in a sneer.

'You ugly sow,' he snarled. 'Hideous, vicious wench. Why don't you lie down and let me kill you? It would be a mercy. For who will ever want you?'

Morwen grinned.

'If my ugliness means I am safe from beasts such as you, then I rejoice in it,' she said. 'Mind where you put your foot, now. There's glass everywhere.'

A crude stratagem, but it worked. Reynardine's eyes left Morwen for an instant, seeking out the shards hidden in the grass. It was all Morwen needed. She drew out her apron and flung it in Reynardine's grotesque face, and as he flailed, fabric clinging like cobwebs to his face, she threw herself upon him.

Her knife found its sheath in his heart, and death came for him so swiftly he did not even have time to howl.

Above them, the whole sky darkened, and the rain came down in torrents.

\*

Morwen looked like a drowned cat by the time she returned to the inn, but Jonty and Marigold were overjoyed to see her, having suffered a thousand anxieties during their vigil. Morwen endured their hugs and exclamations and handed Jonty a leather bag, heavy and clinking.

'There's a small fortune in gold there, courtesy of the good squire,' Morwen told them. 'Enough to get you over the county border and buy a wedding licence, I'd say.'

She smiled at Jonty and Marigold at last, as they embraced one another. She grinned wider as she felt the remainder of Reynardine's gold jingling in her pockets. It may have been grave-robbing, but Morwen doubted she'd lose sleep over it.

*

Having confidently expected his daughter to make a match with rich, handsome Reynardine, Squire Mallinder was scandalised when he learned she'd eloped with Jonty the blacksmith. As for Squire Reynardine, he was never heard from again. But for years after, no villagers would risk walking on the moors when there was both rain and sun in the sky.

Morwen left the village not long afterwards. Whither she was bound I cannot tell you, for even Morwen didn't know. But she felt she had stayed in the village long enough, and now she had a little gold to smooth her way.

Off she went, and she didn't look back. But the villagers often spoke of her, and her brave deeds. In years to come the legend of Morwen and her adventures became so grand that being the Village Ugly was an honoured, sought-after position, for while any pretty girl could be the Village Beauty, only the boldest, bravest, cleverest girls were worthy of being the Village Ugly.

# Dark Glass

by

Louise M M Richards

# Dark Glass

You don't expect strange things in new houses. Old houses, yes. To begin with they make noises that new houses don't. Floorboards shrink and creak, smells seem to pop out from nowhere, and they definitely have echoes, echoes from the past. Many people, after all, have rubbed up against these old walls and left their indelible mark, and people have died in them and waited for burial over several days before funeral parlours and hospices sanitised the process.

So, when Susan Brook agreed to view a modern house because the rent was affordable and near to her tube station and work in South London, she walked into something that was as she expected it to be. It smelt of newly applied paint, its lines were sharp and angular, the colour scheme was monotone with the occasional focus wall, and it was all very clean, in fact, sparkling clean.

It had been the sparkle, however, that had initially caught her eye, and it was not from Windolened bay windows and Flash clean floors, or even high-end black granite work surfaces, this sparkle came from a paperweight, and it was so bright it momentarily blinded her.

When she had recovered from this visual shock, and whilst waiting for the letting agent to finish her phone call, she picked up the paperweight. It must have been left by previous occupants and she wondered why. It was a weighty piece, hand cut she felt sure, with many facets to its surface and probably quite valuable. As she looked down into its centre, she saw what appeared to be an old seaside pier, and there were people in Victorian dress, promenading up and down and generally enjoying the day. As she continued to look, however, she realised that these figures were moving.

She was transfixed by it. And as she held the thing up to

the daylight that was streaming into this bright, modern kitchen, she realised that as she turned it, other pictures began to present themselves to her. For example, when she turned it to the left, she saw a long curve of golden sand that swept around the base of rocky cliffs; there were gulls rising and falling with the incoming tide; and dotted along and down these cliffs were impressive houses of varying types and sizes, all looking outwards and ensuring that any visitor had a fabulous view of the sea. She turned it again. And this time it showed the sails of small fishing vessels intermingling with row boats rocking gently beyond the white spume of the incoming waves.

But as she continued to turn the paperweight, the tone began to change, and another facet showed a much darker scene of an encroaching storm, and the waves that had been hardly an inconvenience to anyone were now beginning to rise up. The same fishermen were shouting at the people in the row boats to return to the beach, but then, with ferocious quickness, the blackness was almost upon the pier, and the wind now so strong that the whole structure shook.

As she turned it again, the sun had come out showing a scene of total destruction. Nothing moved in this picture now. The pier, so pretty a few seconds ago, was a twisted, tangled mess, and the bodies of the elegant promenaders were strewn like flotsam and jetsam across the shoreline, and the row boats and fishing vessels had completely disappeared.

\*

Susan Brook looked long and hard at the paperweight. She had always liked the predictability of the older house that put you on your guard when you entered, and you could either take them or leave them. However, this supposedly pristine modern house had, without warning, placed something cold and nasty in her hand, and she didn't quite know how to deal with it. It was an omen she felt sure, and not just a trick of the light. Still, the rent was cheap for this part of London and it was convenient for work.

After some consideration though, she returned the paperweight gently to its rightful place on the kitchen window sill, shook her head at the agent, and walked away without a backward glance.

# My Son, My Daughter

by

Keris McDonald

## My Son, My Daughter

There once was a woman who tried her hardest to save her child. She lived under the brow of a hill, you see, and on that hill was a copse of ancient trees, and in that copse was a mound with great grey standing stones set about it, and all who lived in the valleys thereabouts knew that sometimes folk came out of the mound and walked this way and that upon the road and the moor. And everyone knew that it was best not to meet these strange neighbours, who searched for anyone they might steal away – but looked above all, with cold hearts and hungry eyes, for little children.

So although her babe was strong and happy, and fed well, this young mother lived in fear. Her husband was a shepherd, often away at night tending his flock and leaving her on her own with the little mite, her firstborn. She knew that if the pastor would only baptize her babe then the protection of the Almighty would be upon her wee darling, but the pastor had been laid up a-bed for months with the dropsy, so they said, which meant he had not been able to christen anyone.

She did her best. She bound rowan-twigs together with red wool to make crosses that she hung from the window frames, and sprinkled lumps of salt and bread across the sills. She hung an open pair of scissors at the cradle's head, like a cross of steel, and the path to their door she strewed with earth dug from the village graveyard. What mother could do more, I ask you?

Her husband, meanwhile, shook his head at her anxieties. 'You've nothing to fear,' he told her. 'I've my good iron axe and my two dogs; I swear by God that nothing will take my brave boy from us.' But his words only froze her heart as they fell upon it, because she had a secret she'd kept from him for weeks and weeks now. A secret that even the midwife, old and half-blind as she was, had not noticed at the birth, and one that was kept swaddled from sight these days. Her purple-faced newborn babe, with privy parts all swollen up, had appeared for all the world like a proud little boy. But when she looked carefully now while cleaning up messes, oh – it was not so clear. A boy's endowment, in part, but a girl's too at one and the same time.

And the young mother did not know what to do, or who she might tell. Would the pastor even baptize such a thing? Would Heaven want her little one? Much as she loved her own, she did not know if her husband would share that love, if he knew.

Lucky it was that men did not change babies' rags.

Then the night came when her husband was away upon the moor rounding up the flock for shearing. The rain was gusty and loud, hissing upon the thatch and rattling the shutters. Near midnight, the mother sat up near the fire and rocked the birch wood cradle with one foot as she carded the last of last year's fleece in her lap and prayed.

There came a knocking, all of a sudden, upon the door. 'Let us in, pet!' It was the voice of an old woman.

She started to her feet. 'Who's there?'

'Let us in! Ach, the night's drear and Aa might perish o' cold!'

The mother lifted the babe from its cradle and tucked it to her breast beneath her shawl, the better to keep it safe and close. She didn't recognize that voice. 'Are you from hereabouts?' she asked loudly. 'Does my husband know you?'

'Nee, pet – Aa'm from a step ower yonder. Ye'll not be leaving an old woman oot-bye to be drowned, will ye?'

Was it her imagination, she thought, or was there an edge of threat in those words? 'It's late!' she cried desperately.

'My blessings tiv anyone who lets us bide by the fire,' came the quavering voice, 'and my curse—'

The mother pulled up the latch before she could finish that sentence. Sure, she knew that the old woman hunched there in the rain was likely no mortal beggar, but the Good Folk of the Mound had their own ways, and it was said that inhospitality in particular raised their ire.

'Come on in and sit by the fire,' she said. 'Warm your bones, old mother.'

The woman was a bright-eyed, silver-haired old body, it turned out when she dropped her sodden coat. Beneath it she wore a dress of white feathers, and the scent of cow-parsley and summer nights came out of that and filled the house. She looked here and there about the room, glanced into the empty cradle, sniffed the air and accepted a cup of new ale before resting her limbs in the mother's own armchair.

'Ye've a bairn, hinny?' she asked, her eyes as yellow and slotted as a goat's as they peered at the bulge under the shawl. 'Aa can smell a wee laddie.' She smiled. 'Let us give him a cuddle, then.'

'He's feeding now,' the mother said, busying herself one-handed with the fire so that she would not have to look at the old dame. 'Let him bide, and I'll make you a bite of supper.'

'What's his name?'

She could not answer that, because the child had not been baptised. She hadn't even picked a name, because she did not know whether it was a boy's or a girl's she should be choosing.

'Does he *have* a name yet?' the old woman asked with a grin. Her teeth were jagged white flints.

The mother shook her head and wondered if she dare make the sign of the cross, and if it would help.

The old woman leaned forward. 'Now then...' she said.

At that moment there came a bump and slither and something spilled down out of the chimney and rolled across the room in a cloud of soot to perch on top of the water-butt. It was as black as ten cats and shaped like smoke; two red eyes glowed like live embers from the darkness. The poor mother shrieked and nearly fell over the cradle.

'How, man!' the old woman snapped. 'What are ye doing here, Gadgie?'

'What cheor, Ganny?' the thing replied, its voice hoarse and dark as its sooty fur. It sniffed. 'Aa smells a bonny wee bairn.'

'Aa was here first.'

'Was. Aa'm here the now.'

'Haddaway and shite. The bairn's mine.'

'No,' said the mother, though her lips were dry as dry. 'The babe's *mine.*'

Her two guests stared at her and the air in the room crackled. 'Aa'll give ye a hatful o' bright silver shillings for your wean,' said the old woman.

'Silver?' she said, and laughed. It sounded screechy.

'And Aa'll give ye a whole pot o' gold, canny hinny,' said the black Gadgie swiftly. She could almost see a man's face, pale and pinched, in the centre of that cobwebbed darkness - but it was like peering down a well a hundred feet deep. 'Not the kind o' gold that turns to dead leaves in the morn,' he added; 'buried weregeld, centuries old. Coins and brooches and arm-rings. Aa'll show ye where it lies, not a foot beneath the soil, down on the river bank. Just give us the bairn.'

'Aa'll make ye rich forever,' Ganny countered. 'Divvin listen to him. Aa'll give ye a wheel that'll let you spin all your fleeces to pure gold.'

'Whisht, ye sweir old biddy. Nee, Aa'll make ye Queen of all the land, bonny lass,' he announced. 'The King hisself will fall in love and marry ye.'

'Enough!' she shouted, startling the pair. 'I will not sell my babe, for all the riches in the world!'

They sat back and glared, somewhat at her but mostly at each other.

'Is it war ye want, Gadgieman?' the old woman asked. 'If ye rob us of what's mine, Aa'll bring war on ye and yours.'

'The bairn's not yours unless the wifie gives it to ye, Ganny,' he growled. 'It's her choice.'

The old woman turned then toward the mother. 'It's only one bairn, and ye'll have others without doubt. Aa'll give ye an ointment that'll take away your cares and years each night, so that every day ye'll grow more bonny and your husband will always love ye.'

'Pah. Aa'll give ye a looking glass that'll let ye see anywhere ye like, all the places of the world, behind every door, even in the secret council chambers of the mighty. Imagine what ye can do with that, wifie!'

'And Aa'll show ye a flower that cures every ill and every hurt, canny lass. It can bring the dead back to life. Ye'll work miracles if ye choose.'

'Is that all? Aa can show ye the secret path to the back door o' Heaven itself, so that ye may pass in and out as ye please, and take who ye want.'

'Stop!' The mother shook her head. It was not that such things did not appeal to her, but she could not give up her child. 'My babe is not for sale, not for gold or for gain. I'm a mother! What can *you* know of a mother's love?'

The old lady stamped her feet in annoyance. 'Aa'll raise the bairn at my own breast then, strong and free and wild, to run with the wind and dance under the stars.'

The shadow man was not having her get away with this. 'Haad on – Aa'll make your child a magus, the greatest seer this land has ever known.'

'Aa'll gift him a horse of moonlight wi'a flaming mane and a harness o' gold and precious stones.'

'And Aa'll... Wait. What did ye say?' The Gadgie paused. 'Did ye call it *Him?*'

'Aye. It's a son at her breast there.'

'Haddaway, woman. The bairn's a wee lassie. Aa know that reek.'

The mother seized her chance. 'I choose, then. I give to you my son, Ganny.' She turned swiftly to the other. 'And I give my daughter to you, Gadgie. And neither of you may take what belongs to the other!'

The shadows swirled and spun around the room and elder-blossom fell from the rafters like snow as they stared and stared at the babe she plucked from her breast, all sleepy and full. The wee thing did not protest as she laid it in the cradle and unwound the swaddling cloths to show them, but just yawned and burped a milky bubble.

White head and dark head bent over the cradle. 'Ah!' said she. 'Hmph!' grumped he. Then they eyed each other suspiciously.

'Ye'll not be laying a finger on what is mine,' said Ganny grimly.

'No more will ye have claim on one hair of what belongs to me,' he countered with a growl.

They both nodded curtly and touched fingertips together, fleetingly.

'As for ye, bonny pet...' said the old woman, turning to tickle the babe's tummy with her bony fingers and making it wriggle. 'Ye are something else, neither and both. Ye will always be your ain sel', nothing less.'

The babe opened its eyes and met her gaze, unafraid.

Then the two visitors vanished into thin air, leaving a scent like marsh-mist and rotting leaves. The mother was alone with the child that she scooped up and held close to her hammering heart.

'My Ainsel,' she whispered, pressing her lips gratefully to that thistledown hair. 'Oh my love, my pet, my sweet little Ainsel.'

And that was how the child was named.

# The Glass Slipper

by

Kim Gravell

# The Glass Slipper

'She did what?'

Claudia stared at her sister in disbelief.

'I'm telling you, she left one of her shoes behind.' Nicole dropped down into the chair opposite, in a flounce of tiered skirts, and put her head in her hands. 'I can't believe it!' she moaned. She raised her head a little, meeting her sister's eyes. 'The Godmother's going to kill her.'

'The Godmother's going to kill us more like it. You know Cindy's her favourite. I tried telling her that the girl wasn't ready to go on a job yet, but she wouldn't listen.'

Nicole nodded sadly.

'It wasn't as though she had to do anything difficult. All she had to do was distract the Prince while we got into the royal bed chamber.'

'Well, she certainly managed that part of the job alright. Although, from the way she was talking when she got home, I'm surprised we didn't bump into her in the royal bed chamber. *The Prince said this, the Prince said that.*'

'*The Prince had his royal hand on my bum all evening.* I know. I couldn't believe the way he was all over her on the dance floor. And she just let him!'

'No class, no finesse.'

'No, but you have to agree she's good with her hands.'

'The Prince would certainly agree. Did you see what she was doing with his codpiece?' Claudia fanned her face. 'Goodness, the youth of today. I'm blushing just thinking about it.'

'All in the name of getting the job done, or so she said, but you could see she was enjoying it. And it was all over the papers this morning. Mystery woman leaves Prince standing at masked ball.'

The two sisters eyed each other. Media attention was not something they courted.

'Thank goodness she made it back to the getaway coach on time,' Nicole said, trying to find something positive in the night's work.

'Only just. Twelfth stroke of midnight is cutting things a little too fine if you ask me. And then she blows it all by leaving traceable evidence behind. Hasn't she learned anything we've been trying to teach her?'

'Buttons won't have had time to fence the jewels yet. All those diamonds; not even the Godmother could make those disappear overnight.'

'You know Sergeant Dandini will have his forensics team busting a gut to trace that shoe.'

'It won't be easy. The Godmother had it handmade.'

'True, but I'll bet there's enough dirt on the sole for them to run a soil analysis and get a good idea of where it's been worn. Plus, Cindy was taking it on and off, on and off, so she could admire it. She must have left her prints all over it.'

'Magic glass, remember? It shouldn't hold prints.'

'Well, I hope for everyone's sake it doesn't.'

'Okay, let's look at this logically. They have the slipper but that's all. The coach was at the breaker's yard within the hour, the coachman and grooms have got new jobs and the horses will have had their coats dyed, their shoes changed and be halfway to a stud farm somewhere across the kingdom border by now.'

'They'll be taking a one-way trip to the dog food factory more like it. And that's where we'll be going if we don't sort this. The Godmother will blame us. You know she will.'

'But what could we have done? The coach had to be out of there by midnight so we could make the drop-off. It's not like we could have gone back.'

'She'll still blame us.'

The two sisters lapsed into gloomy silence. They both knew it was true.

Finally, Claudia stirred.

'What annoys me is how little respect we get. No one acknowledges the hours we spend planning these heists.'

'And all Cindy can do is keep moaning about us sleeping in late and making her do all the housework. If she was out all night casing joints and meeting fences then she'd know how much work goes into these little jaunts she's so anxious to get involved in.'

'You're right. And as for all the complaints about not having fancy clothes to wear. Does she think we enjoy being dressed up like this? I mean, look at me. There are all those lovely shift dresses this season but I end up with all these flounces. I look like one of the Palace Guards in drag.'

'Strong is beautiful,' Nicole reminded her. 'Whereas I look like a clothes mop wearing a wig.'

'Don't be silly, darling; you're willowy. That's why you're such a good cat burglar.'

'Thank you, Claudie. But just once it would be nice not to have to look ridiculous so people don't take us seriously.'

'I'd settle for a conversation where I didn't have to prattle on about marrying Prince Charming. You realise we're going to have to cover for her?'

'What do you mean?'

'Assuming they trace the shoe here – and we have to work on the principle that they will – we're going to have to pretend it belongs to one of us. How tight is your alibi?

'Watertight. My—'

Nicole's answer was cut short by a loud knocking, coming from the front door, followed by the muffled sound of voices. Moments later the family steward appeared at the entrance to the parlour.

'Sergeant Dandini and several members of the Palace Guard request an audience, my ladies. I tried to dissuade him but the sergeant was most insistent that he see you. I took the liberty of showing him and his men into the front salon.'

'Thank you, Randolph. We'll be along shortly.'

The steward bowed and retreated. Claudia and Nicole exchanged horrified glances.

'They can't have traced the slipper here that quickly, surely?'

'They must have. It's either that or someone's grassed on us.'

'Who would do that? The Godmother would turn them into a frog.'

'It doesn't matter. We'll just have to deal with it. Oh, if we don't get arrested I'll have that girl sweeping out grates for a month! You go up to her room and tell her to stay there. Lock her in if needs be, we daren't let her speak to them. Then come and join me in the salon.'

\*

'Why Sergeant, how lovely to see you.' Claudia simpered and fluttered her false eyelashes outrageously as she moved in to plant a kiss on her visitor's cheek. Dandini sidestepped her advance with an ease that spoke of long practice.

'I'm here on official business, madam.'

'Of course you are.' Claudia swatted him lightly on the arm with her fan. 'And you've brought some of your men too. You Palace Guards are so devilishly handsome. It's enough to get me all hot and flustered.'

She raised her fan to her face and then peeked at him, coyly, over the top. Dandini met her gaze coolly.

'I need to talk to you about an item that was recovered from the Palace, yesterday evening.'

The sergeant gestured and one of the guards stepped forward, holding out a plastic evidence bag. The missing glass slipper glistened inside it, sparkling like a handful of diamonds.

'Do you recognise—'

'Oh, you've found my shoe! You sweet man! Aren't you wonderful.'

Claudia flung out her arms and engulfed the sergeant in a hug. He struggled free with as much dignity as he could muster.

'Really madam.' He straightened his tunic. 'Am I to take it that you admit that this item is yours?'

'Well of course it is. Who else would it belong to?'

'It doesn't appear to be your size.' Dandini looked pointedly at Claudia's feet.

Claudia wilted a little under his gaze. Her lower lip trembled, fractionally.

'That's a very hurtful thing to say, Sergeant.'

Unrepentant, Dandini stared at her.

'So why should I believe that this is your shoe?'

'Because it is! Oh alright, I admit it; they don't fit very well.' Claudia treated Dandini and his men to a moue of disapproval as if she had been forced to confess to something distasteful. 'But I saw them when they were in the sales – do you have any idea how much glass slippers cost, Sergeant Dandini? – and I had to have them for the ball, to go with my new gown. I knew they weren't my size but sometimes a lady has to suffer for her beauty.' She gave the men a tremulous smile. 'That's why I changed my shoes just before I left the ball. I just had to; my poor feet were killing me and I didn't think anyone would notice. When I got home and realised I must have dropped one I was mortified. But I should have known you'd come to my rescue.'

She fluttered her fan artfully and was reaching for the evidence bag as the salon door burst open.

'That's my slipper!'

Claudia looked round in horror at the new arrival. 'Really, Cindy dear—'

A breathless and slightly dishevelled Nicole appeared in the doorway behind her. 'Oh, Sergeant Dandini, what a nice surprise,' she said, treating him to a glowing smile as she edged over to Claudia. 'I couldn't stop her!' she breathed to her sister.

'I said, that's my slipper.'

Cindy stood in the middle of the room, her hands on her hips.

'Cindy, don't be silly, darling. You know that's not true. She has such a vivid imagination, Sergeant, and I'm afraid to say that she's always coveting my clothes.'

'You weren't even at the ball, Cindy,' said Nicole. 'Don't you remember? We wouldn't let you go. You told all your friends on social media how mean we were. You should read some of the things she posted, Sergeant. I don't like to use the word ungrateful, but...'

'I was at the ball. That is my slipper and I can prove it.'

'Cindy—'

The sergeant cleared his throat.

'I'm sorry ladies,' (he sounded anything but), 'I'm going to have to take you all in for questioning in relation to a serious crime that took place at the Palace last night.'

\*

There were two coaches waiting on the drive. As the Palace Guards ushered Claudia and Nicole towards the first one, Dandini held Cindy back.

'Not you. You're travelling separately.'

Shocked, Claudia twisted round in the grip of her burly escort.

'Don't worry Cindy,' she sought to reassure the younger woman. 'There's obviously been a terrible mistake, but we'll get things sorted out. Don't be frightened, darling and don't answer any of their questions before—' Her words were cut off as she was bundled unceremoniously into the coach.

Dandini escorted Cindy over to the second vehicle. It bore the insignia of the Palace Guard but closer inspection showed it to be more sumptuously decorated than the first.

'She's all yours, Your Highness.'

Sergeant Dandini handed Cindy up to the man sitting inside. There was a moment's silence as the coach's occupant gazed at her.

'You did it, Cindy! Oh, I've been so scared in case anything went wrong and they suspected you.'

The Prince kissed Cindy's hand but, when he tried to move the kiss up to her lips, she pulled away.

'Oh no you don't, Charming,' she said, giving him a knowing smile. 'You're not getting your hands on my crown jewels until I see that royal pardon we agreed on.'

# Darling Grace

by

Noel Chidwick

# Darling Grace

Your message found me at Tintagel.

I was atop the scaffolding which surrounded the castle in a cage, while builders and bots scurried about the stonework under my direction. I scrambled down the ladders, tripped and stumbled across the cliff top. I clambered into my *Silver Machine*, a teardrop of a craft dazzling in the sunshine. High I flew, heading north east to Northumberland, the green landscape of England passing by a thousand feet below. I raced home to Bamburgh Castle.

I could not enjoy the scenery; instead I sat captivated by the screen in front of me, shivery images sent by your tiny dragonfly released to watch over you. Like you, it was jostled and buffeted by the winds and the waves, but still I could pick out the look of grim determination on your face as you manoeuvred that small boat into the tempest. You spared no thought for your own safety – all you could think about was rescuing those people shipwrecked and stranded on Big Harcar, a slip of an island being eaten by the ravenous tide. I could hear nothing save the monstrous roar of the storm and the crashing of the seas against the rocks. You cajoled the aged engine into pushing the old coble through the cold, grey waters, tossing it – and you – like our dog shakes her blanket in her muzzle.

I sped achingly slowly over the empty marshlands of Somerset, the Isle of Glastonbury shimmering under a crystal-perfect summer sky. Hundreds of miles ahead, you steered the coble ever closer to Big Harcar under swirling, blackened clouds. The storm had blown up from nothing; that morning you had told me you planned to take the boat to Longstone Lighthouse, to visit the graves of your mother and father, to watch the puffins scurrying and fussing. The sea was lapping gently against the shore, stroked by a gentle caress of wind.

Like a daystar I was, blazing over the lush farmlands of Gloucestershire where the corn rippled like golden honey. I was transfixed as you waited for the right moment, at the top of the wave, to leap across to the wet rocks, rope tied around your waist. I yelled helplessly at the screen as you slipped and slithered backwards, only to be heaved back onto the rocks by a wave that threw you contemptuously, like a discarded toy. Somehow, you released the rope, and tied it through an ancient iron ring set in the stone. The shipwrecked passengers stood in a huddle. Like statues. I saw your puzzlement as you pulled your wet lank hair from in front of your face. You approached the nearest survivor, a man dressed in black clothes, a cap sitting loosely on his head. You touched him. He did not react. You pushed him, and he fell backwards, shattering into gravel and sand as he crashed to the ground. His cap stayed fixed to his head, which rolled and fell into the surf. You ran amongst the others, each as unreal as the first, and they all crumbled at your touch. You shouted at the sky and your tears mingled in the salt-spray hitting you in the face like tiny hammers on an anvil. It was some moments before I realised that these shipwrecked sailors were identical.

My *Silver Machine*, your wedding present to me, sailed over the urban wastelands of Birmingham, now a desolate museum to former mad times. The sun beat down on me through the cockpit canopy. A flock of geese, the V shape-shifting in the currents, passed over me in a flicker of shadows. I barely registered them as I called out to you, uselessly, futilely. Through your dragonfly's microphone I heard the banshee howling of the elements of air and water, turbulent, crashing over you, aching to hurl you into the cold depths of the North Sea. Then I saw you reach into the pockets of your skirts, wrapped around your legs like pleading children. You brought out your reality wand, the unearthly metal shimmering in its sheath of latticed leather. 'No!' I shouted. Your wand should have been secure in the castle vault – you had *retired*, your work was over. You stumbled; felled by a fierce gust of rain-sodden wind as heavy as a sack of seed potato. Slowly, you managed to get back on to your feet. Your dragonfly held steady, and I could do nothing as I watched your fingers manipulate your wand, the cold making your movements clumsy and stiff. As the tide threatened to engulf you on the diminishing perch of stone you looked into the little camera – at me – and I made out the words, 'Please forgive me, my love.'

Of course I forgave you.

\*

*The Reality Shifters saved humanity. They took their wands of MacIntyrium, manipulated them and all around them reality changed. The Reality Shifters fought the forces that nearly destroyed the Earth in their orgies of greed and consumption, and gradually, over many decades and generations, almost beyond perception, like the movement of a minute hand on a clock face, a blanket of sanity and peace settled over the world. Their task was thankless, and they tried to remain from view – shadows behind a veil – but there are still those who think they were the villains, shaping the world to their own form. The disasters and the slaughter of billions of human lives and the near extermination of life on this planet – all now a distant memory. I didn't know that you, Grace, were a Reality Shifter – one of the last ones.*

*You returned to Bamburgh where you were born and lived as a child. I was looking for my next project, and there was Bamburgh Castle, still imposing and strong overlooking the North Sea and the nearly drowned Farne Islands to the east, and the village at the foot of the Castle Rock. You bought the decaying castle and I was the engineer chosen to oversee the reconstruction.*

*I loved you from the first. Your long black hair seemed to nestle around your shoulders like a purring cat, and your smile, gentle and giving, drew my heart to you. I spilled coffee on the plans and you mopped it up, your face close to mine. I stared into your eyes of deep, cool jet, and I could see the faint lines that talked of horrors witnessed. You traced an outline of the stain with your finger and laughed, 'See, you've brought the tide in to the castle.'*

*We were married a year later in the village church and we moved into the rooms at the top of the castle, while work continued on returning the King's Hall to its stately glory, a magnificent display of armour, swords and pikes.*

*It was on our first night together when you took me down to the Keep. You told me who you were, what you had been. You showed me your wand; I'd never seen Macintyrium before, and you giggled as I tried to hold the mirror-bright metal baton. Of course I couldn't hold it – its very lack of friction gives it away as not being totally of this reality. Its weight too: an element heavier than all other elements. It slid out of my hands and slithered along the stones. We laughed as we finally cornered it, and you carefully manoeuvred it into its leather sheath. Then you showed me how to manipulate reality.*

\*

I shook myself free of my thoughts and returned my attention to the screen. I watched in despair as you twisted and turned the wand, moulding reality ever so slightly, just as you did that night. The winds gradually eased, the rain stopped. The waves settled down like lambs at their mother's side. A glimmer of sunlight pierced the clouds.

'I think I know who did this,' you told me through your dragonfly. 'I need to get back to the castle. Come as soon as you can.'

'Yes! Yes!' I called, even though I knew you could not hear me.

You jumped into the coble, and fired up the engine. You steered the boat artfully away from the rocks.

Below me the terrain turned to woods, forests and the glittering strands of canals; the long cargo barges threading along them in their own time.

You raced across the water, heading towards the jetty below the castle. The wind was blowing favourably, and the currents too seemed to be on your side, and even as my cocoon of metal carried me over the pastures of South Yorkshire, I watched you beach the little boat and run up the dunes, slipping in the sand and the grasses.

Your boots click-clocked on the cobbles, and your skirts skittered about your ankles, hitched up in a clump in your fist. I'd never seen you this intense. Who was it aimed at? Who in the castle would fill you, my love, so full of hatred? You heaved your body into the huge oak door, the wood darkened by hundreds of years, but shining with nurture and renewal. Up the stairs you hurried.

I urged my machine onwards. The North Yorkshire Moors, apportioned out by walls of stone, undulated below me.

You crashed into the King's Hall, large windows gazing out to the islands and the horizon beyond. There was a man standing there, his back to us – Grace and her dragonfly viewer.

'Jorme Urnstrong!' you called, and raced at the man. He

turned. I recognised him – not by name, but by his face. The face that Grace smashed into the rocks in the storm that nearly drowned her.

'Get out of my home!' you shouted. You saw something in his hand. The dragonfly swooped around, and I saw the unreal shimmer of a fragment of Macintyrium in a crude sheath of leather. 'It was you! You created that storm, you wanted me to die out there, smashed and drowned on the rocks!' I could hear Grace's voice, shrill and fierce. Who was this Jorme?

You reached in to your own pocket. You drew out your wand. 'But you didn't expect me to have this with me, did you? Why did you do it?'

'Why?' His voice was a deep growl. 'Why? Because it should have been mine. I should have become a Reality Shifter. It was down to you and me, you didn't even bother to show at the end. And then you come back here and pretend not to know me.'

'Who is this Jorme?' I shouted. Only Reality Shifters had wands: was he a colleague? A friend? I began to think that I had seen him before.

'This castle should be mine – it belonged to my family once.'

'This castle was a ruin until my husband and I restored it.'

'Aye, with money made by your distortions.'

No. No! I watched him begin to twist his wand.

'And you shouldn't have that wand. How did you get it? Did you steal it? Give it to me before you hurt anyone.'

'No, lass it's mine – I made it myself.' Jorme lifted his wand high from your reach – you looked so much like a frightened bullied child, my love. 'Fragments and nuggets, blasted together in my furnace.'

The blacksmith! Jorme was the blacksmith. He'd turned down my offer of work on the castle.

You continued, trying to take the wand from him. 'How did you learn how to use it? It's dangerous. You have no idea of the damage you could have done to us all.'

'I learned, little Gracie, I've learned an awful lot. I may not be as slick as you and your precious Shifter friends, but I can still work it. It's not as difficult as you all try to claim. I'll show you. Maybe I'll show you what you think I am.'

Jorme twisted the wand in his hands with ungainly, yanking movements. The room filled with smoke – shadows and shapes of what I could not tell, and I could make out neither you or Jorme.

'Forgive me again, my love,' I heard you utter.

'No! No! Forgive me for not being there for you now!'

Below me, the Tyne sparkled, smoke spiralled up from farm buildings dotted along the river, Newcastle now a village of a few thousand inhabitants.

\*

*We talked long into the night, and you explained how you worked, shifting from one reality to another. Many times, you said, you inhabited realities where the air was thick with the stench of death and decay, where living things starved and suffered. Humanity was a stunted thing, slaves and overlords together. You had to find where goodness and badness mingled and disentangle them, slowly teasing out the threads to restore the beautiful world. Years of training, closely watched. You suffered; you had to see the alternatives, watch death march over nations, see the atmosphere turn foul, the water turn putrid, see huge rainforests wither, burn and die. You lived through it, and lived through it many times. Then, you knew anger, anger at what humanity had done to itself, and to the world. Anger you learned to tame, to control, and you used that anger to turn reality away from that dark road, and onto a new path glistening with promise.*

*At last, you could do no more. You told me that there comes a time when every Reality Shifter has to stop; the anger can be controlled no more. You stopped. You needed rest. You found it in Bamburgh; you found love with me, and I with you.*

*I looked at you anew, my love. The terrors you faced, the choices you made, the loves you found and been forced to abandon. You and the other Reality Shifters sacrificed nearly all you knew to save the world. I loved you all the more.*

*You snuggled into me, the scent of your night-black hair sweet in my nostrils. You took my hands and showed me how with a twist of the wand here, and a touch there, you could make reality do what you wanted. You conjured a moth out of thin air, small and yellow like a buttercup hovering between us. It flew out of the bottle-shaped doorway into the sunshine. I held you, and you turned in my arms and looked up, your palms pressed against my chest. We kissed.*

*Looking out over a peaceful and calm world now it is hard to believe the evils of the twentieth and twenty-first centuries ever happened. And now the wands were to be put away and kept safe: changing realities to save the world should not need to happen again.*

\*

The smoke, like smudged particles of reality, spiralled in on itself and formed a hideous troll-like figure towering over you. His fists were as big as boulders, though he still clutched his wand, peeking out between fingers of scabbed flesh. He took a lumbering step towards you.

'Is this what you think I am? Some kind of monster?' He swung his arm.

I saw your hands take your wand. A stroke, a caress, a tiny gesture and the wand bent to your design. The fog returned, and there was a scream that turned to a howl that turned to a roar. The fog vanished, and the images on the screen shifted and darted. You transformed. I saw a massive, swirling golden tail, huge claws with savage talons; and a long, lithe body of leathery scales with a dragon's head of ferocious red eyes and jagged teeth. The Jorme-monster was felled by one sweep of your mighty tail; he crashed onto his back in a cascade of flying furniture and falling armoury. 'Grace, please no!' he cried, as you towered over him, a she-dragon protecting herself and her life. You snatched at Jorme's hand, and ripped the wand from his grasp.

By now I had bid the machine to drop, and it landed smoothly on the beach, to nestle in the dunes. I raced up the same steps that Grace had ran up a few minutes before. With my palm I slammed the emergency button in the porch to summon help and I clattered into the expanse of the King's Hall.

I paused, breathing hard. I had to take care: when a Reality Shifter is working her wand, distortions can ripple out like waves and capsize anyone caught unawares, drowning them in uncharted realities.

I saw you in all your power. 'Grace!' I called. As Grace-dragon you had backed Jorme into a corner where along the wall ran a display of 17th century pikes. You turned as I called. You bellowed at me, my love, and I saw your teeth sharp as knives.

Jorme took his chance. He pulled away a vicious pike that had not been used for four hundred years and speared you in the heart. You heaved yourself away, your cries filling the Hall; the spear clanked to the floor.

You half crawled-half scrabbled away, but your forearms were still nimble enough to work your wand. There was an explosion of that same unearthly fog and it enveloped the Jorme-monster. He writhed and screamed, and there was a sickening sound of crunching bones and gristle. And there sat a grey toad, the size of a cat. As Dragon-Grace you leapt on the Jorme-toad, and glided down the steps to the Keep with the creature held tight in your talons. I followed – I nearly slipped on the pools of blood on the stone steps. I was too late to interfere as you pushed away the iron grating to drop the toad into the well. There was a deep splash a few moments later.

I ran over to look down, but it was too dark to see. Then from behind, another swirl of fog, warm as fire, swept past. I turned.

'Ben, help me upstairs.' You were a dragon no more. Blood formed a circle like a blot of red ink, spreading over the silver and grey stripes of your dress just below your breast. You clutched at your wand and I carried you up to our rooms, your pale face and sweet lips close to mine.

You spoke. 'I'm sorry, Ben. I should have been more prepared.'

I lay you down on our bed.

\*

Between gasps and washes of pain you talked in fragments. Later I pieced it together. Jorme was at school with you when the Testers came. They were looking for suitable children to nurture to handle the Reality Wands. They settled on deciding between Jorme and you, but you missed the final tests while you looked after your father that day, the day before he died.

You have to be good to be a Reality Shifter. The person who instinctively helps; the one who puts other people before themselves. After all, you are altering the fate of millions of people and a planet. Jorme wasn't chosen.

In you they saw that goodness: in Jorme, they saw ambition, they saw greed. The Testers took you away to your new life.

But like the gunslingers of the wild west, there is always someone who thinks they are sharper than you. Jorme, seething with resentment was that someone. When you returned, many years later after all you had done, he saw you in the village. He spoke to you, but you had forgotten him. But why should you have remembered him? It was so long ago, a different world. He returned to his furnace.

You never told me; if only you had told me. But after that you took your wand from the vault and kept it with you.

I held you tight, tried to warm you, your skin turning cold. Breathing was hard for you now. I ripped your dress, pressed on the wound, my hand red with your blood, your life, seeping out. Why was no one coming to help?

'Your wand! My love, use your wand!'

You grimaced, shook your head, a tiny movement. 'Can't change this. After. Someone else. I love you, Ben.'

As you spoke, words dripping out slowly, you took your wand, and twisted. 'Only chance. Love. You.' Your next breath was your last. I pulled you to me, rocking, shaking, squeezing, holding. I kissed you, tasted my tears and the sea and your blood. I buried my face in your hair and held you, trying to cage your spirit, to keep you with me. Your hand opened, and your wand fell heavily to the floor, a sparkle in the fading light.

I don't know how long I sat there with you limp as a rag doll, but footsteps, heavy boots on the polished wooden floor caused me to look up. It took a few seconds for me to take in what I saw. Dripping, his jeans and jacket sodden from his escape from the well, but human, stood Jorme. He was big, powerful, the arms of a true blacksmith, and taller than me by a head. His face was grazed, blood dripping into his right eye. He seemed not to notice. He smiled.

'She's dead then.'

'Bastard!' I shouted, and leapt at him. I hurtled into him, head straight into his stomach, and I shouted and raged. I punched and kicked and brought down this mountain of a monster, until he regained himself and smashed me in the side of my face with a fist as big and as hard as a stone from the castle wall. He didn't need to be a troll to overpower me.

I rolled over, dazed. Beaten, I lay on my back. He stood over me, frowning.

'You loved her,' he said.

'She is my wife,' I said. My blood now mingled with yours on my face. I eased myself up.

He was peering down at your face now, beautiful, serene even, in death. The creases drawn by the terrors you had seen had gone now. You were at peace.

'Grace has done so much to save this world, you would never know.'

'Is that what she told you?' said Jorme. 'These Shifters. Saving the world by changing it. It's their world, of course, not ours. *Their* perfect world.'

I wasn't listening. You were dead. My Grace was dead. My glorious, wonderful, dearest Grace was dead.

'I can bring her back to life.'

'What?'

'I can. This metal of hers. I can bend it, and bring her back. And she knew it.'

'Please don't joke. Don't. Don't make it worse.'

'No, I can.' He bent down to pick up your wand. The drips from his sodden jacket made little ripples in a small pool of your blood. 'See? Her wand. It's been set. You can't tell, but I can. And she knew it. That's why she turned me back.'

Grace? Did you? Is that what you meant? Is that what you meant by 'someone else?'

'I need a while to prepare, but aye, I think I can do it.'

'The police are on their way. The ambulance is on its way. They should be here.'

Jorme laughed. 'No, they're not coming. We're in our own bubble of reality here; Grace made that, not me. I can tell. She's left us alone for me to bring her back. She was a clever woman. That gives me time. Time to think. You'd better leave me with her.'

'No!'

'Listen – Ben isn't it? If you want me to bring her back you'll have to trust me. I'm not the wizard she was, I'm just a knuckle-dragging Smithie. It'll take a while, and it might not be pretty, but I think I can do it.'

'Why?' I asked.

'I've killed her once. That's enough.'

'Yes, yes, bring her back, and we'll not do anything to you.'

'No, you won't.' He frowned, turning your wand slowly, peering at it closely. 'Go wait somewhere else.'

What choice did I have? Without you, my love, my life would be as empty as that shell of Tintagel Castle, but with no one able to restore it. Maybe Jorme could; maybe he would. I had no choice.

I made my way to the kitchen, splashed cold water over my face, over my hair. Spirals of red circled the plug hole.

I sat at the table, feeling the wood under my fingers. I pushed the chair back, scraping over the stone. I went to look out of the window. It was darkening outside, and a single seagull called over the sound of the surf washing gently over the beach below. The tide was receding, the sand was smooth, a fresh canvas for footsteps and dog prints. Longstone Lighthouse was shining in the twilight, a minute passing on every third blink; the clouds of a real storm were brewing on the horizon beyond.

At last, Jorme came down the steps. He leaned against the doorjamb, head down. Beads of sweat glistened on his forehead.

'Is she alive?' I asked.

He didn't answer, but looked up at me strangely, as if he wasn't sure who I was. Then a flicker, a flicker of recognition.

'That took some doing,' he said.

'Well?' I asked again. 'Is she alive? Tell me!'

He nodded. Smiled. 'Aye.'

'Thank you! Thank you!' I was thanking her murderer, but I didn't care.

'Aye, she's alive, as you asked, remember. Took some doing, that, took some working out. She's alive.'

I pushed past Jorme, ran up the steps.

\*

'Grace!' I called. You were standing – standing! – at the bedroom window looking out at the same lighthouse, watching the same storm now lashing down over the white waves crashing on to the beach below.

I ran to you, you turned. I reached out for you, to wrap you up in my arms, to hold you, feel your warmth, your body, smell you, taste your hair, see your smile, hear your voice whisper in my ear, feel your heart close to mine. But you pulled away, scared, puzzled.

'Jorme!' you shouted. 'He's here! Stop him!'

'Grace, what are you doing? He killed you!'

'Jorme!'

Jorme came up from behind, and pulled me back; I couldn't get out of his grip.

'It's okay, darling,' Jorme said. 'The police are coming. They'll take him home.'

Your look of fear and revulsion – at me! – hurt me more than the punch from the blacksmith-troll.

'What has he done to you?' I shouted. More boots on the stairs, more arms strong, authoritative. I was dragged away. 'Grace! Grace! Stop them!'

I was hauled from the bedroom, dragged through the King's Hall – away from you my love – and out of the castle doors. I crashed down onto my knees. The rain pounding on my head.

'Just take him home, officer, I think he's just been drinking again.' Jorme spoke calmly to the policemen as they pushed me into the back of their vehicle.

'Certainly, your lordship.'

Jorme returned inside, where I could see your silhouette framed in the firelight behind you.

I heard the slap as loud as a thunderclap, watched your silhouette crumple to the floor. 'That's for turning me into a toad!' The police officers closed the car door in my face and we drove down the drive and through the gates.

I haven't seen you since, my love. Jorme returned your life to you; he'd twisted reality but now the reality was his to control – Lord of Bamburgh accompanied by his elegant Lady Grace.

The police took me "home", the shack behind the old walled garden at the other end of the village. I was kicked and pummelled out of the car and left bleeding in the road. I wanted to die, Grace, I wanted oblivion, to be washed away in the river of rain and down into the sea like a dead branch from a tree.

I crawled out of the road and into the shelter of the wooden shed and found a pile of cardboard and rags in which to burrow, and hugged my own pain away.

Fragments. Shattered pieces. My "new" life came to me, a

tramp living off scraps and tiny acts of kindness in a world full of noise and squalor and the stench of a sick society. Wars and famine; even here in little Bamburgh there is a brutality tearing at its soul, and the feared Lord Jorme reigns over his manor with a grip as tight as the one he once used to wield a hammer. The world of peace that you helped shaped, Grace, was gone as if it never happened; which, in this reality, it didn't.

Next morning, as the light of dawn seeped over the dismal horizon, I recovered my silver machine, still resting in the dunes. I hid it in the ruins of the church, destroyed in a fire years ago. Where we were married two years ago. I remembered your words when you gave me this wonderful machine. 'It is always yours, no matter what.' I realised then; I should not remember those words, should not remember our life together: what did you do to me? To my machine? Was this your insurance?

\*

It has been many months, now. I managed to remove the MacIntyrium from the heart of the machine (why did I not question how the machine was powered?), and, in the dead of night, I have practiced and twisted and shaped my improvised wand. You taught me well the basics, even though you should not have done so. I have two lives playing in my head: our life of love together and this sour world forced upon us. I am going to banish this second nightmare that should not be, and restore our life together. I look up at the castle at night, and see the lights in the windows. I fear what Jorme is doing to you, my love, but I will make it right. I will leave this distorted half reality, and take you with me. I will learn how to manipulate our realities and restore the rightful one – for the world and for you, my Grace, my darling Grace.

# Chantress

by

Aliya Whiteley

## **Chantress**

I sing for the sake of singing. They provide me with subjects to sing about, but my desire is only for my own sound. I don't think they understand that.

I am the Chantress. I'm not to be confused with the Enchantress who lives at the top of the mountain and soothes the stars, night after night, with her pleasing, persuasive speeches. I should also not be mistaken for the Disenchantress who lives at the dark pit of the valley below and mutters if you happen to pass within hearing distance. She is a warning – a demonstration of the depths to which a disobedient woman might sink. She is also responsible for occasionally throwing rocks, and directing white and black flies to the nearest vegetable plots.

That's just my little joke.

The women from the village on the far side of the mountain come to me, making the trek on the precarious path their ancestors carved, and I'm quite clear with every application that the songs I'll form do not have a purpose, in the sense that no song has a direct purpose, but this has yet to stop them from asking. They say, 'Sing a song that will make my child better.'

'The child probably needs a doctor,' I say. Every single time. 'I'm no doctor. I have the number for the surgery in the town a few miles away, and the opening times for the cable car that will get you down the mountain. Also a bus timetable. Here.'

Sometimes they accept this information, sometimes not. Every time they say, 'Sing it, please. Sing it anyway.' They are so reluctant to leave the shadow of the mountain.

\*

*Child, stay close, and find your comfort*
  *In the strong tall peak above you,*
  *Formed by the Giant Hands that cradle*
  *That mould*
  *That shape*
  *That close about you now*

\*

I find comedy in the strangest things: the crooked legs of the dead insects on my windowsill; the lost goat hanging on the ledge, bleating, amazed to find itself in such a precarious situation; the skittering of loose pebbles on their way to the valley below. I put it down to being alone for so many years. I say so many years – six, to be precise. I moved here from the town, after seeing the job advertised in the local paper.

*Do you want to SING for a rapt audience?*

I thought, after years on the circuit, doing the working men's clubs and struggling to be heard over the clink of glasses and roar of innuendo, that it had been placed there purely for me. We make such connections, all of us. We assume there is reason to events, and a thread that runs through our souls and tugs us this way, that way, onwards, with the far end of the thread held firmly in Giant Hands. It's much easier to think that. It gives each life a meaning that I'm not sure it deserves. Still, it worked in my favour this time. I attended the audition in the fervour of certainty. It was my chance to shine, as they say.

I discovered, while standing in front of a row of bearded elders who had agreed to reimburse my bus and cable car costs, that I could improvise with tune and lyrics. They liked the sound of my voice, and the words I chose. They told me – *Come to the village and guide the women of our village. They need your voice.*

How they auditioned the Enchantress and the Disenchantress, I don't know. I should remember to ask my sisters, during one of our quarterly meet-ups.

I sit on the roof of my village-sponsored hut, with a glorious view of the heavy mist that shrouds the mountain peaks; the usual drizzle is headed my way. The Enchantress, high above me, will have a clear view of the sky, which is necessary for her role. The village believes stars are little girls – the giggling children of the sun and moon – who must be gently addressed by a soft voice. She does this well, and with dedication.

I don't sit here for the view. I get the best wifi reception up here, on my antique of a mobile phone, having been out of contract for five years and eleven months.

I scroll through the headlines.

The news is busy consuming itself, as usual. How important it must seem to those who consider themselves part of that cannibalistic mechanism.

*Next up: a report on the deadly disease sweeping the city – news addiction.*
*Further updates on this breaking story by the hour.*

Not really. I made that one up.

There go some pebbles, dislodged from the path, and then I hear the footsteps approaching, and a firm knock upon my door, three times, as per the custom.

I quietly climb down from the roof on the far side of the hut, and then walk around to my own front door with the dignified air that is expected of me.

'Can I help?' I say to the villager. She's tall and thin, wearing her hair in a series of complicated long plaits. She's too young to be here about her child, so this must be a visit about the second biggest issue that concerns the women of the village.

'Chantress,' she says. 'Please. I need a song. A song to make a man love me.'

I invite her in, and sit her down, and explain very carefully that the song won't work. She nods, and nods, and then says, 'So will you sing it?'

\*

*A good strong heart calls to yours,*
    *And you dream of better things*
    *but where will you find them?*
    *In the sky?*
    *Look up, and see the work of Giant Hands*
    *About you*
    *Around you*
    *For you.*
    *They weave clouds from tears*
    *So cry for what cannot be:*
    *feed the clouds,*
    *then find solace in the good strong heart*
    *that is waiting*

\*

Why so many ill children and unrequited love stories? I confess, I do not know. It perplexes me. I harbour theories:
- The village is an experiment run by unscrupulous scientists who want to see if it is possible to regress human achievement

back to a Stone Age; the mist of the mountains is actually a powerful gas that works by shrinking the frontal cortex.
- The village doesn't exist at all, and this is an elaborate hoax being played upon me as part of a television programme that airs nightly to the amusement of millions of people. All the villagers are actors. Some are better at acting than others.
- The village has always been my home and everything before, including phones and nightclubs and bus services, has been created by my sick and troubled imagination. And I'm obsessed with sick children and unrequited love. In short, I'm mad.

I could pick one of my theories and stick to it, but instead I like to roam free, siding with whichever one suits my mood. Right now I'm mad. I'm enjoying the broadening complexities of the word. Also, there's a lot of room within my job specification to play madness. The villagers seem to like it, too. It suits their image of me – the things I say and the way I am.

*

'Mine's burning,' I tell her.

'That's okay,' says the Enchantress. 'The outside gets a bit black, but the inside is still yummy. I can't believe you never did this before.'

'It wasn't that sort of childhood,' I say. I remove my stick from the flames and examine the charred, gooey mess of marshmallow. It has ash stuck to it.

'Seriously, it's delicious,' she says. 'Pop it.'

'I'm not popping it. It's too hot to pop.'

A stone is flung out from the darkness; it smacks into the bonfire and dislodges the tent of sticks, which sends up a plume of smoke and cinders, and a wave of heat. I put my hand to my face, and feel my cheeks, awash with it.

'Just chill!' shouts the Enchantress, and from behind a large rock nearby I hear the Disenchantress mutter, and move off. She'll do it again in a minute or two. She really cannot divorce herself from her job any more. When we first began these meet-ups she would join in with the normal conversation, and even say amusing things, droll things, every now and again. That hasn't happened for at least a year.

I nibble the marshmallow, and taste smoky sweet strangeness. It's not like any other taste. I'm not sure that I like it, but that doesn't matter. 'So how's your mother?'

'It won't be long,' says the Enchantress, throwing back her head. 'I can't see the stars from down here. What a relief. Even when I was back in town, getting her moved to the hospice, I'd find myself outside at dusk talking to them. My girls. The stars, I mean. It's just habit. It's all become a habit.' I glance up too, and see the smoke rolling skywards, making its own mysterious, curling patterns before succumbing to dissipation. 'When she really starts deteriorating they'll call me, and I'll try to get back in time to say goodbye. I've said it anyway, though, just to be sure.'

'Said what, sorry?'

'Goodbye.'

'How did you do that?' I ask her. I can't imagine it – such a huge thing done at the wrong moment, as a failsafe, simply to make sure it had been done. A rehearsal, perhaps, that might have to be the stand-in for the real show. I never said goodbye to my own parents, not in that way. They're still out there, ongoingly doing parental things; I'm sure of it.

The Enchantress shrugs. 'It's just a word.' What a strange thing for her, the weaver of words who soothes starlight, to say. I watch her pop her own marshmallow, as if the heat does not affect her, and then she skewers a new one on the end of her stick, taken from the plastic packet beside her. 'You want another one?'

'Yeah, okay.'

She passes me a white one, and I eat it straight away. It's better cold, I think: soft and dense, intact, soothing in my mouth.

'You're not meant to do it like that,' she says. She gives me another one, and I spear it on my stick, to make her happy.

'Thanks for sharing these,' I say. 'I keep meaning to take a trip to town. It's been ages.'

'What will you bring back? When you go?'

I try to picture what it is I most want.

A stone flies out, again, and smashes into the fire. The Enchantress takes a marshmallow from the packet and throws it, with violent energy, into the darkness. There is a pause. Then the muffled voice of the Disenchantress floats forth.

'Thanks,' it says. 'Tasty.'

'Where's your family, anyway?' says the Enchantress, clearly proving her determination to switch the spotlight away from herself, whether I answer or not. But these are not the kind of questions I like.

'Oh, I don't have a lot to do with them,' I say. 'They don't really understand me.'

'You don't speak to them at all?'

'It's fine. They're farming folk, from the other side of town, beyond. They think I should still be there, milking the cows, and that's not me, is it?'

Her attention is fixed on the fire; the slow settling of the embers after the disruption of the stones. 'I don't know if that's you,' she says. She drops her stick, stands, and lifts her arms to the sky.

*I see you, stars, little girls of light, I see you hiding, peeking out from between the fingers of Giant Hands, and you don't know if we want you to adorn our lives with your bright, fair light because we are so busy down here, too busy to look up and tell you so. But you are wanted. You are loved, little dots, tiny twinkles. You are wanted, and you will be much missed if you do not come out tonight. So find a way to slip through, we beg you. I am the mouthpiece of the village. I stand at the highest peak and wish I could hold you close, closer. You delight me, stars, with your ageless patterns and delicate beams; I would kiss you, if I could, and wrap myself in you. But I can't. And that's for the best, because you're shy. I know it. I see the way you hide in the Hands. Come out, stars, come out. Slide through the giant's grasp, and keep us all in your glow tonight.*

The Disenchantress mutters, close to my ear: how did she get so close? This time, for the first time, I hear every word.

*You work so hard and nobody really appreciates it. Not one of them. What difference does it make? What difference does it all make, anyway? Pointless. Bloody pointless.*

'I know,' says the Enchantress. 'It's just habit.' She sits down again, and we finish the marshmallows, and then start the slow climb back up the mountain to the roles we keep on playing.

\*

'You are the Chantress?' says the frowning young woman. She falls into none of the usual categories. I don't know what she wants, and what's more, she's caught me at a bad time; I'm fresh from washing my hair, and am in my dressing gown. I don't look the part, and I don't feel it. I shouldn't have answered the door, but it didn't follow the usual pattern of three knocks, and I was curious. Perhaps it was someone else.

A person from outside the village.

'If you'll just wait, I'll get changed and be with you—'

'No, please, I wish to speak with you, that's all,' she says, so I have no choice but to open the door wide enough to admit her. She stands in my hut and looks around, as if searching for something other than the simple furnishings. 'They've always said, my mother says, you're from the town. Chosen.'

How stilted she sounds. Do any of the villagers have a sense of humour? I've yet to find it. 'Yes, I was.'

'Didn't you bring any of your own possessions with you when you came to us?'

'Not really.' What things did I have? I think of the phone, of showing it to her, but I don't like the way she's making me feel. I'm being judged, and showing her the phone would be an attempt to prove myself different. 'Did you want a song?'

'What good would it do?'

'None.'

'Because there's no such thing as the Giant Hands?'

'That's right,' I tell her.

'Yes,' she muses. 'That's what mother told me you would say. You saved my life once, she thinks. It was when you first arrived. I was fifteen. I had a fever that wouldn't break, and you sang for me. Over me. But I don't think it made a difference. I think I survived because I'm strong. Stronger than any imaginary hands, high above.'

Nothing about this is going the way it should. I haven't moved from the door; it's still open. 'Listen, you go out and I'll get dressed, and then when you knock again I'll be ready to do this the proper way, okay?'

She doesn't move. She says, 'I'm leaving the village. I cannot be bound up in these old superstitions about stars and songs and stone-throwing. My mother made me come here, to see you, before I go.'

'Does she want me to sing a song that will make you change your mind?'

'Maybe.'

'Where will you go?'

'The cable car. Then the bus.'

'I have timetables,' I offer.

'I don't need help.' She moves past me, and out of the doorway, to stand in the grey morning light. No doubt it will rain later, but the air is clear, that much cannot be denied. Even if there is no sunshine, the air is clear and fresh and free. She will miss that, at some point, even if she doesn't believe it now.

'I'll sing you a song anyway,' I tell her. 'That's what you really want, isn't it? Everyone does.'

She shakes her head. 'Don't sing to me. Your songs: they do work. But not in the way that you think.'

And she sings instead. She sings to me:

*Why must you fight*
*Your reason for living?*
*You are the Chantress:*
*Your voice, your thoughts, your heart,*
*Your soul, have been poured into this life*
*by Giant Hands.*
*Do not look up to the stars:*
*they are not your domain.*
*Do not cast stones and threats upon those who need you.*
*Sing, Chantress, sing.*
*It is your gift, made for giving.*

She has a good voice. It's not as good as mine, but still, there's something haunting to the melody.

'Goodbye,' she says, and sets off, on the rough path. I

watch her go. I think about following her, catching her up, and going to town together, to start afresh. But I'm not like her, not any more.

I am the Chantress.

There's nothing out there like it, and nothing could be as important. I wish I could make a joke of it, but I've run out of punchlines. I, and my fellow employees, have work to do here, for those that believe in us. You might say we are sisters. We are in the care of Giant Hands.

# The Art Glass Paperweight

by

Marija Smits

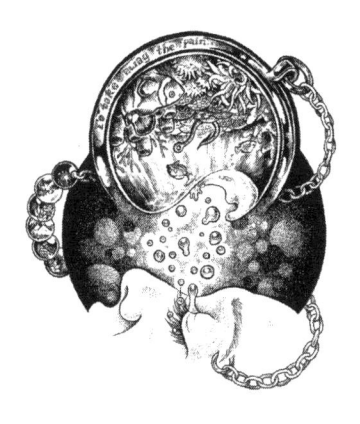

# The Art Glass Paperweight

Once upon a time a golden-haired woman, heavy with child, sought out a man skilled in the art of magic. She told him that she was in love with a bad man, a man who beat her, and yet she couldn't leave him. She asked the magician to take away her crazy love for the bad man. The magician said that he would, in return for her most precious thing. The woman looked down at her belly and the magician said, 'Yes, that will do.'

\*

Vanessa dried her eyes on her dressing gown and then picked up her notebook and pen. She took a sip of tea and then wrote the following:

*Tariq*
*Andrew*
*Paul*
*Krishan*
*Steve*
*Nikesh*
*Steve (again)*
*Riz*
*Ben*

She paused, tears blurring her vision, and then finally managed to write: *Robert*.

She wiped her eyes again and began to add more detail to the list:

*Tariq – together for 6 months. I was still madly in love with him when he dumped me. Spent the following 6 months in utter misery.*

*Andrew – together for 2 years. Fell out of mad love with*

*him after about a year, but was hoping to settle down with him. That is until:*

*Paul*

Vanessa continued with her task. When she got to the end of the list she shut the notebook and shoved it into her bedside cabinet, suddenly disgusted with it and herself.

Was this how the rest of her life was going to play out? Was there always going to be mad love followed by misery? Or mad love followed by a comfortable sense of ennui, and then "another" who would make her fall madly in love again.

What she really wanted was to be *permanently* out of love. Because when she was in love (or its reverse: misery) she wasn't able to think properly, or concentrate on her work, let alone finish writing the novel she'd been working on for the past three years. Yes, she wanted to get married one day, start a family, but was all the love-madness, pain, and trial-and-error relationships worth it?

Vanessa forced herself out of bed and to the bathroom. A month ago she and Robert had planned on going to the Nottingham Contemporary today, to look at the new art exhibition. So what if they weren't together anymore? After lunch, she would go by herself. She turned on the shower and decided that yes, today would be the first day of a new life. A life without love.

\*

**The magician trapped the golden-haired woman's limerence in a glass ball so that she no longer loved the bad man who beat her and was able to leave him. When she gave birth to her son the magician found her and wrought his magic, turning her son into a living work of art.**

\*

The art in the gallery did not hold Vanessa's attention. So she left the concrete cubes, illuminated balls of string and paintings that didn't amount to much more than random daubs of paint to go to her favourite coffee shop, the one on Market Square.

After her coffee she wandered along the busy streets towards Lace Market. A tiny jeweller's caught her eye, the sparkling gemstones winking at her. She slowed and then went to the shop window. Second hand rings, antique brooches and necklaces all gazed up at her.

Vanessa sighed. How often had she dreamt of that moment when her one true love – what rubbish that was! – would invite her into the shop: 'You know, to see if there's something you'd like?'

She tried out a smile; she could cope.

Anyway, why shouldn't she buy *herself* a something? A symbol of her commitment to a life without love. She took a deep breath and then entered the shop, the bell on the door announcing her arrival.

A middle-aged woman with hair the colour of cement was sitting behind the till. She was polishing a silver candlestick, her vacant eyes on a lottery ticket on the counter. She hummed a tuneless song.

Vanessa looked down at the jewellery beneath the glass counter. She particularly liked the art deco rings – the one set with a princess cut emerald was stunning, but so was its price.

The sound of steps made her look up. The beaded curtain at the doorway behind the counter parted with a clicking swish and a man emerged through it. He looked as though he was straight out of an Agatha Christie story. He could have been either detective or villain, with his moon-like face, receding hair and neat moustache. A monocle, bow tie, white shirt and waistcoat completed the look.

'Can I help you?' the man asked, his accent strange. It seemed to be part German – or part Dutch? – and part Nottingham.

'I'm just looking,' Vanessa said dismissively, wondering what kind of man was pretentious enough to wear a monocle in this day and age. She gave him a cursory smile and then looked away.

She felt a sudden twist in her neck – a trapped nerve? – and her head jerked round to face the man. His eyes bore into her and she felt claustrophobic, as though he was somehow invading her mind.

Words tumbled out of her. 'I want to buy myself a present.'

The man nodded and then gave her a sickly smile. 'We have lots of beautiful things,' he said. 'Not only beneath the counter.' He indicated to the shelves on the wall.

They were full of strange objects. Glass spheres that contained swirling, sinuous strands of colour, brass skeleton clocks that were made out of other clocks, mirrors with mosaic frames. There was even a glass dome that contained a fabulous paper sculpture made out of pages from a book.

Vanessa gazed at the objects. Not only were they beautiful, they were exquisitely made. Looking at them made her feel... joyous.

'That glass ball?' she said, 'The one that's full of coral and fish. How much does it cost?'

'Take a look,' said the man, reaching up to get it for her. 'It is an art glass paperweight.'

Vanessa turned it over in her hands. It felt warm and somehow alive. It was incredibly intricate; there even appeared to be tiny, ghostly faces within the globe, floating amongst the glassy reef. And when she looked at the bottom of the paperweight, she read the faint, etched words: *To take away the pain.*

'What does this mean?' she asked.

The man smiled, though his eyes did not. 'It means that it takes away the pain of love. Or whatever you like to call it: limerence, madness, obsession.'

Vanessa's eyes became round. This was ridiculous. 'And how is it supposed to do that?'

The man ignored her question, picked up the paperweight and put it back on the shelf.

'But it's not for sale,' he said, his eyes flicking momentarily to the woman at the till. 'It's for safekeeping.'

'Then why,' she said, trying to keep the anger out of her voice, but failing, 'did you show it to me if I can't have it?'

The woman-at-the-till's humming droned on. It made Vanessa want to scream.

The man said nothing and instead took a clear and colourless glass sphere from beneath the counter.

'But you can buy this,' he said. 'And by the pain etched on your face, I can tell that it will become even more beautiful than the other paperweight.'

'What do you mean? How does this ball become like the other one?'

Momentarily, the jeweller was there again, in her mind.

Vanessa wanted to protest at the intrusion, but before she could he was out of her head and she was sure she must've imagined it. The jeweller told her to touch the glass ball.

She did so and memories of her time with Robert rushed out of her: their first date – anxiety chewing at her insides as she waited for him at the left lion, the sky grey, the people grey. The sudden fear that Robert, new to Nottingham, might not know what stone statue she'd been talking about. Then, spotting him amongst the crowd, his orange beanie bright amongst all the grey, and feeling as though the sun had just come out. At the radical bookshop, browsing the titles on display. Exchanging glances. What books should she plump for? What would impress him? Eating ugly bread from the artisan bakery, their hands almost touching as they tried each other's filled focaccias. She and Robert at the lake, messing about in a boat. Their first kiss in the quiet lane that ran along St Mary's Church. Long, delicious nights at her flat when they'd hardly left the bed. Croissants with jam for breakfast. Then the awful non-response to her messages; the final heartbreaking text that told her he was seeing someone else. Vanessa wanted to cry.

Robert's face began to appear in the glass and Vanessa peered at it, amazed at the likeness. How was this impossible thing happening? Vanessa felt the pain lessening, her tears subsiding. She felt a peace that she hadn't felt in weeks. It was wonderful.

'Do you see?' said the jeweller, whisking the glass ball away from her. 'It takes away the pain of love and fashions it into something exquisite.'

The pain was back again and Vanessa found herself wiping away a tear. 'I understand,' she said, suddenly sure that she had to have the glass paperweight whatever the price. 'How much does it cost?'

At that moment a fair-haired young man, carrying several bags of shopping, came into the jeweller's. He went straight to the woman at the till.

'Think I got everything,' he said. 'D'you want a tea, Mum?'

The woman shifted her gaze from the lottery ticket to her son and then nodded, her tuneless hum unbroken.

The young man went into the back of the shop, the beaded curtain clacking behind him.

'The cost?' said the shopkeeper, as though nothing had happened. 'This cannot be bought with money. You must pay me with your most precious thing. A necklace, perhaps? Or watch?' He looked into Vanessa's eyes again, searching. 'A book. A diary.'

She thought of her notebook. It contained most of her novel and her "love" confessions. 'Okay...' she said, slowly weighing up the bargain. 'I can do that. When do you close?'

'Soon,' said the man, his monocle glinting in the lights. 'Come back on Monday.'

Vanessa sighed. 'Okay,' she said, 'Monday.' She then left the shop, the bell tinkling after her.

\*

Peter, the jeweller's assistant, looked at himself in the bathroom mirror. It wouldn't be long until he would be wearing another face – he'd been through the process of metamorphosis enough times to recognize the signs of approaching change. It was a pity really, as he quite liked this pale, slender face.

Tears came to his blue eyes. He blinked them away, suddenly noticing that his eyes were more brown than blue.

Today he didn't know who he hated most: the magician-jeweller or his mother.

'Are you happy?' he remembered asking her a while ago.

'Yes,' she had said. 'The jeweller gave me the gift of calm. A life free of the turbulence that comes with love.'

'But what is it that makes you happy?'

'You. My work. Watching my soaps and doing the lottery.' She had sighed. 'I'm only sorry that your life is... difficult.'

'Do I make you happy?' he had wanted to shout. 'Because it doesn't seem as though you give a shit about me. Or anything. You don't feel a thing.'

He had wanted to shake her, to hit her; to make her feel pain.

Instead, he'd thrust his hands into his pockets and hung his head.

His mother had patted him on the shoulder. 'Don't worry about me dear,' she had said. 'I'm fine, honestly. Just fine.'

Peter suddenly heard his name being called. It was dinnertime.

He left the bathroom and trudged down the stairs, his blonde hair becoming darker with every step.

\*

On Monday, Vanessa returned to the jeweller's with her notebook, more sure than ever that she wanted to be rid of the pain (and ecstasy) of love. She'd had a productive Sunday, writing the whole day. If she continued in this vein her novel would soon be ready to send to agents.

When she entered the shop she'd expected to see the woman, but instead there was a young man in her place. He had tawny-coloured skin and curly black hair.

'I'm looking for the jeweller,' she said.

Peter went to the doorway and called for the magician-jeweller, who came almost instantly.

'You have your precious object? Your book?' said the jeweller.

Vanessa passed it to him and he leafed through it.

The jeweller looked up at her. 'You do understand that this book can never be returned to you? It will be turned into something else. And sold.'

Vanessa nodded. 'I understand.'

'Very well,' said the jeweller, passing the clear glass paperweight to Vanessa. 'Keep it close to you. Hold it often. It will take away your pain.'

Vanessa clutched it to her chest and smiled. 'Thank you.'

*

The son of the once golden-haired woman grew into a fine, young man, though his metamorphic body kept him in the shadows of the city, unable to lead a full life. One day he happened across a notebook and fell in love with the words of the writer, who was a butterfly of a woman. But he knew that the woman would be unable to love him because she'd been numbed. The magician had trapped her capacity for limerence within a glass ball. Still, he yearned for her and one day set out to find her.

*

It took Peter ten months to find Vanessa.

One afternoon he went to her place of work, the Lakeside Theatre, and waited until he saw her. He asked if she'd mind speaking with him. He had something important to say.

She looked at him with vacant eyes, unable to place him, and said okay, she'd talk to him, but she couldn't stay long. She'd had a tiring day and wanted to get back home.

They went to the small gallery space and sat and stared at the photographs.

'So what's all this about?' she asked.

'You have a paperweight,' he said. 'An art glass paperweight, with a whole world inside it.'

'How do you know about that?' she snapped.

'It happened by accident, I swear. But before the jeweller turned your notebook into a sculpture, he left it open on the table. I saw it and started to read. Once I started, I couldn't stop.'

'So what? You read my stupid novel. And random scribbles.'

'But it wasn't stupid. I can't say I know much about books, but your novel... it was beautiful and arresting. And so full of love. It made me want to know you better.'

Vanessa laughed. 'It was a shitty first draft. That's all.'

'And what you wrote, I mean, not in the novel, but about how you longed to settle down with someone who really loved you. And to have his baby. *To breathe in its newness and feast on its milk-sweet love.*'

Vanessa wanted to laugh at what he'd just said, but she was unable to. Hearing her words from his mouth was... unnerving.

'The others,' he continued, 'who came to the jeweller, to have their limerence taken away. I don't know about them all but, well, I think that from reading your notebook you made a mistake.'

Vanessa thought about her art glass paperweight. She had once thought it beautiful, with its rays of sunlight, birds and clouds, the ghostly faces. But not anymore. Now it simply sat on her dressing table, gathering dust.

'Did you ever finish your book?' asked Peter. 'Get it published?'

Vanessa shook her head. 'I... I haven't had time to write.'

'Why not?'

'You know,' she said with a shrug. 'Work. Netflix.

'Besides,' she went on, 'what's the point? There are thousands of other writers out there. What have I got to add that's so special?'

Peter shook his head. 'Like I said, I don't know much about books. But I want to ask you this: are you happy?'

'Happy?' she said with a snort. 'Happiness is for the idiots who get taken in by advertising companies.' She sighed. 'But I'm okay. Content. Isn't that enough?'

'Maybe,' he said. 'But shouldn't there be more to life than just being content?'

Vanessa stood. 'I've got to go.'
'Of course,' he said. 'But maybe I'll see you around?'
'Maybe.'

\*

When the metamorphic man found the butterfly woman she didn't care to hear what he had to say. But he came to her again and again. He promised that he'd always be good to her. And with his many faces he'd always be what she desired. Together, they would thwart the magician by finding happiness with each other. The butterfly woman thought about all that he'd said and one day wanted to know what it was like to be in love, for love was everywhere and all around her, and yet she could take no part in it. So one day she smashed her art glass paperweight. It was then that she was able to see the metamorphic man with eyes attuned to love. And only then were they able to begin to live happily ever after.

# Notes on Stories

# About 'Pelt'

I've always been fascinated by fairy tales, particularly ones with animals. 'Red Riding Hood' is my favourite. It's a story I can see with closed eyes, a world of contrasts. Red. Green. Young. Old. Fur. Skin. I started 'Pelt' with these pictures in mind. I'd been working on a story about 'Hansel and Gretel' for radio and started this at the same time. They all connected to a feeling I had.

I'd won the *Mslexia* Short Story Competition with a story about a woman who tells the Grimm's folk tales. The story was called 'The Story that was Never Told'. I wanted to do a whole collection of short stories that were never told, the fairy tales that got away. The strange stories fantastic women live, but may never even whisper. This story was one of these fairy tales. I finished it when I saw the call-out for this anthology. I loved writing it. It's an afterwards story, a life that continues when we think the story is done. It has only just begun.

Fairy tales often play with the idea of disguise. The true self is cloaked, to be revealed only when someone has earned a glimpse of it. The servant who is really a beauty, the beast who is truly a prince. 'Pelt' springs from this place. The narrator plays the role she feels she is supposed to. The sweet old lady, grandma in her cottage, knitting to satisfy the expectations of her family. Beneath that, she is something more. There's a wildness in her nothing can tame, not even age. There is no going back once we have seen inside the wolf.

**ANGELA READMAN**

# About 'The Glass Legs (or it's easier than you think)'

'The Glass Legs' came to be in October 2017. I had challenged myself to write a short scene or story every day of the month, for a list of thirty-one single word writing prompts. The prompt for October 24th was 'breakable'.

I wrote the opening scene of 'The Glass Legs' off the top of my head. After writing it, it was apparent to me that Audrey was a woman disguised as a man; that she had romantic feelings for Cordelia; and that Cordelia reciprocated these feelings, but did not yet know consciously that Audrey was a woman.

I found this scenario so tantalising that I revisited the story later in the month, writing for the prompt 'invitation' the scene where Audrey reveals her gender. I didn't know what happened in between the two scenes, but I knew I had to connect the dots.

It wasn't until I finished the story that it was apparent to me that I'd written a sort of inside-out Cinderella. Here it is the "prince" who disguises herself to attend the ball to meet and rescue "Cinderella".

But if Audrey is the prince, she is also the fairy godmother, her criminal skills and ease of shifting identity its own form of "magic". The story takes place in a world where sorcerers and magic are commonplace, but Audrey's independence and freedom from gender and sexual norms are "impossible".

And as the Fairy Godmother gave Cinderella her glass slippers, Audrey gives Cordelia control over her glass legs, and by extension, gives her back control of her destiny.

To me, Audrey's shifting identity and the freedom it affords her represents the freedom from gender and sexual norms that lesbians and bisexual women have historically enjoyed, quietly and under the radar of heterosexual society; as Audrey puts it, *'the way a woman loves a woman, when no one is watching.'*

**KATIE GRAY**

## About 'People Will Talk'

Gossip is a powerful thing. It can change the way that people look at you, the way you are treated and the way you think about yourself. It can have a profound effect upon your self-esteem and mental wellbeing. It can have a catastrophic effect on your entire life.

Gossip is a powerful thing. Fear of gossip can be overwhelming.

Worrying about people talking about you, especially if you have a dark secret, can overtake your entire life. Life stops being about living and starts being about maintaining the pretence. This leads to stress, anxiety and can cause depression as you desperately try to maintain the illusion while part of you hopes that the whole thing was over and you could move on with your life.

In 'People Will Talk' Amanda's life has become about maintaining the illusion of her perfect life. She's rich, famous and has a wonderful husband. And she's miserable. She's bored and frustrated and she's tired of hiding the truth. The disintegration of the fantasy life everyone else sees her leading has become almost inevitable.

Recently I was told that people cannot identify with science and fantasy fiction as much as other genres because other genres are about life and emotions and being human. I laughed and said that nothing is more about being human than science and fantasy fiction. The hotel on the moon and the robots in 'People Will Talk' are just a bonus. 'People Will Talk' is about Amanda and Dominic's lives and emotions and what it means to be human. It is about human behaviour and human society.

The fact that everyone in the story isn't a human in the biological sense is irrelevant.

**DONNA M DAY**

## About 'The White Wolf'

A year ago I got some feedback that the best part of two stories I had submitted for the last *Forgotten and Fantastical* anthology was the way the wolves that featured in them had been written. It was coupled with a request – please write more about wolves. I spent the next few months sulking because the wolves were not meant to be the stars of those stories. I also spent them developing several stories featuring wolves. I've never been able to resist a challenge!

My favourite of the stories I wrote was 'The White Wolf'. It's a simple story but there's something about it that gives me shivers when I read it – even though I wrote it. It didn't take very long to write the first draft, and this was one of those rare stories that I was almost completely happy with straight away. During the editing process I made some very minor changes to the storyline but mostly just proofread. Even after I followed the famous advice of putting it in a drawer for three months and then re-reading it I still couldn't find much wrong with it.

A lot of people have themes and deeper meanings in mind when they write a story, but when I try to do that the story inevitably ends up terrible. So this story doesn't have a deeper meaning, it's just a story. That means you can take from it whatever meaning it has for you. I hope you find something in it that speaks to you.

**SARAH HINDMARSH**

## About 'Princess, Star, Brilliant'

There has been a thread of story running through my whole life, despite many knots and tangles along the way. As a child, my grandmother read me fairy stories, and I discovered the joy of being transported to other worlds via the magic of words. It wasn't long before I started telling my own tales, starting with teeny books I created for my dolls. They were good listeners.

Fairy tales spring anew for every generation. I can't get enough of retellings where princesses rescue themselves. But what about those who refuse to rebel? My story tells of two sisters: Emerald and Diamond. One chooses to escape her claustrophobic and dangerous family. The other not only chooses to stay, but locks the prison door from the inside.

Using the image of gem cutting, I explore how we can force ourselves into unnatural shapes – both physical and mental – in order to achieve a self-destructive ideal. As we know, the thing about perfection is that it's unattainable. We always fall short, whatever lengths we go to.

There's a gruesome image near the end of Grimm's version of Cinderella, where her sisters cut off their toes and heels in a desperate attempt to fit the *impossible* glass slipper. What strikes me is what women faced with limited choices will do to themselves to reap the limited rewards on offer. When grabbing a husband is the only goal to which women are told they can – or ought to – aspire, they mutilate themselves in order to "fit".

Not that I have any intention of preaching. I'm not a fan of people banging their fists on the table and telling us what we ought to think. Probably because of all the church sermons I had to sit through as a kid. To quote Tom Clancy, I want to tell the damn story.

To break free and live free is tough. There are losses

involved. I don't gloss over the hard work needed to escape from the magic castle. However, I retain a sense of understanding and empathy for those like Emerald who choose to remain, even at a terrible cost. And I leave the reader with hope. Diamond shows how it's possible to break free from the shackles of expectation and make a way in the world.

**ROSIE GARLAND**

# About 'Fossils'

I co-run a young writers group in Bradford Central Library on Wednesday afternoons. Impressions art gallery is housed in the same building and sometimes we visit to draw inspiration from the exhibitions. This isn't ekphrastic writing (a straight description of the art work). Instead the art is the starting point and we use various activities to encourage individual writers to develop their own responses. If the group are in the flow, we write too.

So it was that we entered The Jerwood/Photoworks Awards 2015 exhibition, sat on the floor in front of Tereza Zelenkova's work and began to write in response to her black and white photographs of Eastern European woods. I've always felt beckoned by woodland settings, which I see as being simultaneously frightening and magical, of this world and of the land of the fairy tale.

I like to access an art work directly without the mediation of the artist's biography but, reading up on Zelenkova now, I find she's interested in mysticism and the landscape of the former Czechoslovakia. She mentions fantastical short stories that have influenced her work. There is a satisfying cyclicality to that because Zelenkova's photographs lend themselves to narrative. 'Fossils' also draws in shadows of traditional fairy tales, folk ballads and the inimitable Angela Carter. According to Guggenbühl, fairy tales can help children learn how to deal with "dark forces" (p.7-8). I took my theme from one of the age-old dangers young people face, now in sharp relief thanks to social media – the emphasis on superficial ideas of beauty.

Over the course of three years, I worked on 'Fossils' while it sought out a magical path. You're invited both to follow its winding way and to stray into the woods of your own imagination.

Guggenbühl, Allan. *The Incredible Fascination of Violence: Dealing with aggression and brutality among children,* trans. Julia Hillman. Woodstock, Connecticut: Spring Publications, 1996.

**BECKY CHERRIMAN**

## About 'Human Point-oh'

If you have a keen eye for technology, you might remember having gone through your own 'Human Point-oh' style transition in the autumn of 2013 or thereabouts, a time when half the world's smartphones changed their software to a new version that had a very different design from before. As with most updates to that system, it proved to be utterly irreversible. Once consented to by the user, the update could never be undone.

Indeed, my inspiration for writing this just so happened to be from a personal device I have refused to update for six years, and I used it for the first four of those. It had a lot to do with the way the older version looked, and even now, I find it retains a certain charm – virtual buttons that look as if they have the sun's light shining on them – which today's minimalist blank canvases don't even try to replicate. If I could be said to have had any overarching aims when writing this, it was to reflect on the subtler costs of technological progress. Even before this, I had some plans to put these themes in practice for the challenging genre of high fantasy, and I may yet revisit these plans if I get the time.

But if I had to guess, then perhaps the biggest reason this story resonated with other people – who aren't necessarily as enthused with technology as I am – is because it could equally be read as a parable for many other things, like demographic change, and how one copes with the death of their own culture. We preserve things for as long as it makes sense to preserve them. And when we can no longer do that, we put them in museums. 'Human Point-oh' laments this change, but it makes no attempt to override it. The protagonist of this story is well and truly left behind by what happens to the rest of humanity, but never does the story try to suggest humanity as a whole can avoid this change, nor even that they *should*. The morality of this is left up to the reader.

**JONTY LEVINE**

'Human Point-oh' was first published in *Open*, a limited edition Nottingham Writers' Studio booklet in 2015.

## About 'The Fox's Wedding'

My story sprang from several sources. One is a song by one of my favourite musicians: 'Blood Red Sky' by Seth Lakeman. It's about a mysterious character named Reynardine, a man who is also a fox, a shape-shifter, who preys (naturally) on beautiful young maidens. Another element was learning that in Japan, when it's raining in one part of the sky and sunny in another, it's referred to as 'a fox's wedding'. And another was getting thoroughly sick of adjectives such as 'lithe, slender, delicate' and 'lissom' used to describe women's physical appearances in fiction. All of these combined resulted in 'The Fox's Wedding'.

Reynardine (not to be confused with the famous French folkloric fox Reynard) is a comparatively recent addition to British folklore, first appearing in the early 19th century in a broadside ballad. Like most foxes in folklore, he's cunning, sly, and presumably lives outside the law. His predatory interest in young women suggests that he's an inheritor of a much longer fairy tale tradition of demonic bridegrooms, a vulpine Bluebeard. Upon learning this, I wondered what would happen if a woman fought back, and my story began there.

My heroine, Morwen, is unbeautiful by the standards of her society, and deliberately so. I think fiction in general is guilty of paying feminine beauty too much attention – would Tess of the D'Urbervilles have led such a dramatic life if she hadn't been beautiful? Almost certainly not! Morwen doesn't need beauty, because she's tough and clever and adventurous. I also wanted her to remain separate from Reynardine's games of seduction and flirting, and the simplest way of doing so was to make her plain. Reynardine is an unreconstructed misogynist, and because of Morwen's lack of looks, Reynardine overlooks her until it's too late.

Shape-shifters are among my very favourite characters in

fiction, and my own stories feature them regularly. It's rare for me to present one as unabashedly evil, but Reynardine is intended as a (not terribly subtle) reminder of how easy it is to allow looks to deceive, instead of looking a little deeper, as Morwen does.

**CARYS CROSSEN**

# About 'Dark Glass'

This story was initially prompted by a paperweight brought into my writing class by my writing tutor. The picture from within it showed Victorian couples promenading along a pier.

I had always been taken with a tract from 1 Corinthians and the idea of looking *'through a glass, darkly'*. Varying meanings and translations have been attached to the King James version of this biblical passage and most have (unsuccessfully in my view) attempted to improve upon it. The words themselves are beautiful and enigmatic, and writers such as Agatha Christie and Sheridan Le Fanu have made literary profit from them, which has helped to bring the words forward into common usage.

As human beings living within an often puzzling world, we cannot always fully understand what it is we see. The idea of a multifaceted glass paperweight that provides a number of possibilities as to what could happen if we embark on an innocent trip to the seaside for example, is meant to put us on our guard, and becomes a metaphor for the pitfalls of life generally; and we either heed these warnings or we don't. The protagonist in this story, like the rest of us, wants to feel secure in the house she chooses to live in, but doesn't fully understand the significance of what she has seen in this modern house and feels tricked by it. For her it would be the older house in which ghosts and secrets are expected to lurk and play their nasty games, which in turn makes us wary.

As with most of my writing, I seek to question the acceptable and to move the reader away from the stereotype to another realm. Every day I look through my glass darkly and am always unsettled by what I see.

**LOUISE M M RICHARDS**

# About 'My Son, My Daughter'

'My Son, My Daughter' was inspired by my favourite traditional fairy story, 'Ainsel', and functions as a sort of prequel to that if you like, depicting Ainsel's very early days.

The traditional story (of the 'Self Did It' type 1137) comes from Northumbria in the North of England, and the clever escape depends upon a pun in the local dialect. So when writing this I decided to give my fairies North-Eastern accents. My own mother and father come from Newcastle so I had fun playing with the wonderfully evocative and earthy Geordie vocabulary, though I didn't quite stretch to "Haddaway woman man," my Dad's most fondly recalled phrase. Apologies for any dialect mistakes I've made!

I've run LARPs revolving around British fairy folklore, and written several erotic novels drawing upon it, and I've always tried to remind people that pretty isn't always good, nor ugly evil, even in fairy stories. The Fair Folk are deadly dangerous in both guises, and not to be judged by appearances.

I also wanted to write about a child that could not be pigeonholed as male or female and is therefore entirely an individual in their own right, with unrestricted potential. I definitely look female but I've never really felt that it's an integral part of my personhood. If I'd been born thirty years later than I actually was, I might be identifying as non-binary now. Oh well... one of the functions of story is to explore possibilities and might-have-beens. Maybe I'll return to Ainsel in fiction at some later date.

**KERIS MCDONALD**

## About 'The Glass Slipper'

The original stimulus for my reworking a fairy tale came from a competition in a popular UK writing magazine. I have no idea why the dark recesses of my mind threw up the idea of the Fairy Godmother as the head of a crime syndicate but from there it was no great leap to having the glass slipper as a piece of evidence in a criminal investigation. And that was as far as it got. *Maybe for next year's competition*, I thought and – like many of my writing ideas – it got parked, awaiting that semi-mythical future day when I would have "time" to work on the story properly. I jotted down a few notes to remind myself of my idea and then forgot about it.

Fast forward several months and I found myself at FantasyCon, listening to a panel session on myths and fairy tales. Talking to Teika at the Mother's Milk stand afterwards, she told me about the anthology. I mentioned my take on Cinderella and she suggested I should buy a book and submit the story. A clever sales pitch perhaps, but fortunately it came with the happy ending of her liking the story enough to include it in the anthology. However, that moment was still in the future. At the time I spoke to Teika, I hadn't yet written the story, but here was my incentive to do so. As in all good fairy tales it was completed – if not on the stroke of midnight – at least on the afternoon of the 30th November deadline.

The conversation between the two sisters came to me very quickly. I could hear their voices and sense their frustration in the roles that convention forced them to play, as well as their understanding that they were going to have to step in and save their ungrateful younger sibling from the consequences of her own incompetence. The second scene, with the Palace Guard, took a little more thinking about and hence there are more details to accompany the dialogue. But the outcome still wasn't clear to me. Would Cindy burst in to claim the slipper as her own? And, if she did, what would happen next? As I often do when faced with a character refusing to cooperate, I went for a run and – somewhere between miles five and six – the answer and the final twist came to me. I hope you enjoy it.

**KIM GRAVELL**

# About 'Darling Grace'

I wrote this story while on holiday in Northumberland. For many years I've visited the majestic Bamburgh Castle overlooking the immense sandy beach to the east, and the wee village at its foot on the other side: it is one of the most atmospheric and inspiring places to explore. That it's also where Grace Darling lived and died just adds an extra touch of romance. I've always wanted to write a story with Bamburgh at its core.

Reality puzzles me. The question of what the Universe is was the main reasons for studying astrophysics, and we seem even further from an understanding now – dark matter, dark energy – crumbs, there is even a theory that our universe is no more than a holographic projection of... something.

A few years ago I wrote a series of short stories based around a 19th century Edinburgh academic who discovered a new metal that allowed the wielder to manipulate local reality simply by twisting a small bar of this new element: it was named MacIntyrium after its discoverer Professor MacIntyre. What a power! Michael Moorcock's gods were Lords of Law and Chaos: just imagine MacIntyrium in their hands.

Back in Bamburgh I was reminded of the Ballad of the Laidley Worm, in which a jealous stepmother turned a Bamburgh princess into a loathsome serpent. The ballad and its many variations tell of a battle of shapeshifting through various members of the animal kingdom, and in one version a blanket.

Quietly contemplating the big open sky over the North Sea to the Farne Islands I threw the fragile nature of reality, Bamburgh Castle, The Laidley Worm and Grace Darling into a pot, and hurled it into the future. This story climbed out of the wreckage and looked up at me with big brown eyes. 'Write me,' it said.

**NOEL CHIDWICK**

# About 'Chantress'

My inspiration usually turns up in the form of a moment of description that comes to me, and 'The Chantress' had two such moments long before I had worked out what was going to happen in terms of a plot. A woman was sitting on the roof of her small house, high up in the mountains, checking her mobile phone. And two women were sharing marshmallows around a campfire, in the same mountains, while a third prowled in the darkness around them. The only way to find out why these images were bothering me was to sit down and write a story that linked them.

China Miéville's novella *This Census-Taker* was definitely sticking in my mind when I created the first draft, as was Joanna Spyri's *Heidi*, but on top of those visions of a remote, elevated escape from urban complications I also wanted there to be a reminder of ground-level life, of a modern normality that can't be truly forgotten about no matter where you choose to go. Cable cars and the bus timetables sneaked into the story, along with family commitments and news bulletins. They are links to the towns, the cities, where nobody's singing songs to keep the stars in place or conjure giant hands.

Inserting lyrics directly into text has been something I've experimented with before. I like the direct way that lyrics can speak to the reader here, and also the warning the story contains about believing in persuasive songs, or stories, without evidence. I think I ended up telling a tale of a woman who wants to find importance and glamour and truth and meaning, and thinks all of those things should somehow be related. So she's high in the mountains and down in the town, and not quite anywhere in between.

**ALIYA WHITELEY**

# About 'The Art Glass Paperweight'

'Limerence' is a word that was coined by the psychologist Dorothy Tennov back in the 1970s to describe an 'involuntary romantic infatuation for another person' – an experience that many humans know all too well. It is also known as 'person addiction' since the experience is accompanied by intrusive thoughts, rumination, and an almost obsessive need to have one's feelings reciprocated. Some people simply call it 'love'.

When one's limerence is reciprocated by this "person of our dreams", what a blissful state of affairs that is! But what if – as in 'The Art Glass Paperweight' – that person doesn't love us back, or purposefully hurts us when we're in such an emotionally heightened and vulnerable state?

Being a limerent myself I'm all too aware of the sometimes blissful, yet sometimes excruciatingly painful, feelings that limerence arouses. There have been times when I've wanted to erase it from my life, but then I wondered if perhaps, for all its emotional upheaval, it was a creative force for good? If this was the case, would I trade it in for emotional calm? Probably not. Though I can't help wondering what conclusion others may come to.

**MARIJA SMITS**

# Index
## of Writers with Biographies

**Becky Cherriman** (p. 59)
Becky Cherriman is a writer, workshop leader and performer who works part-time in creative writing community development at the University of Leeds. Her short fiction has been published in anthologies including *The Forgotten and The Fantastical 1*, shortlisted for The Fish Short Story Prize and displayed on umbrellas in Grassington Market Square. Her poems have been published by Seren, *Mslexia*, *The North*, and Bloodaxe, commended in the Forward Prizes 2017 and longlisted for The National Poetry Competition 2018. Becky's poetry pamphlet *Echolocation* is published by Mother's Milk and her collection *Empires of Clay* is published by Cinnamon Press. www.beckycherriman.com

**Noel Chidwick** (p. 117)
Noel Chidwick is Editor-in-chief and co-founder of award winning *Shoreline of Infinity* Science Fiction Magazine. Noel's a lifelong science fiction reader and fan, meeting his hero Isaac Asimov back in 1974. He co-edited the Birmingham Science Fiction Group fanzine before heading off to study astrophysics at Newcastle University. He continued north to Edinburgh in 1981 – where he has lived ever since. For many years the day job was teaching in Further Education, and his other lives were: editing a folk magazine; playing in ceilidh bands; running an indie music publishing company; singer-songwriter with his prog-folk-scifi band Painted Ocean and playwright. Owned by wife Jane, two children and Rosa the Red Setter. www.shorelineofinfinity.com  Twitter @noelchidwick

**Carys Crossen** (p. 75)
Carys Crossen has been writing stories since age nine and shows no signs of stopping. Her first academic monograph is forthcoming from University of Wales Press and her fiction has been published by Mother's Milk Books, Dear Damsels, Cauldron Anthology, Drabblez Magazine and others. She lives in Manchester UK with her husband.

**Donna M Day** (p. 41)
Donna M Day is a writer, actor and director who lives in Liverpool, England. She writes flash, science and fantasy fiction, and poetry, and was awarded Ink Pantry's Inktober Award for Prose in 2016. She runs acting and writing workshops and performs regularly in the north west region. She cooks (well), sews (mediocrely), draws (badly) and can play two whole songs on the piano (both with one hand).
www.donnamday.com

**Rosie Garland** (p. 53)
Rosie Garland is an award-winning writer of fiction and poetry, and sings with post-punk band The March Violets. With a passion for language nurtured by public libraries, her work has appeared in *Under The Radar*, *Longleaf Review*, *Mslexia*, *Butcher's Dog*, *Ellipsis*, *The North*, *New Welsh Reader*, *Rialto* and elsewhere. She's received writing commissions from Brontë Parsonage Museum and Tate Modern as well as nominations for the 2018 Pushcart and Forward Prizes.

She's written three novels: *The Palace of Curiosities*, *Vixen* and *The Night Brother*. *The Times* has described her writing as "playful and exuberant... with shades of Angela Carter."
http://www.rosiegarland.com/

### Kim Gravell (p. 107)

Kim Gravell lives a dangerous life which is to say she has an artery-clogging, deskbound job with a global technology company compounded by a writing habit which leads to her spending even more hours chained to her PC. She is the author of two paranormal adventure novels – *The Demon's Call* and *Child of the Covenant* – and is currently finishing a third.

Kim lives with her husband in mid-Wales. She loves travelling, people watching and animals of all shapes and sizes and can no more imagine spending a day without writing than she could a day without breathing. For further information on Kim and her writing please visit kimgravell.com.

### Katie Gray (p. 21)

Katie Gray is an author of science fiction and fantasy based in Scotland. She has a masters in creative writing from the University of Edinburgh. Her work has appeared in *Freak Circus*, *Microtext 3*, an anthology from Medusa's Laugh Press, and in *Shoreline of Infinity*, Scotland's dedicated scifi magazine. Her short story '3.8 Missions' was reprinted in *Best of British Science Fiction 2017*. She is currently working on her first novel, a YA fantasy about wizards in Victorian England. When she's not writing, she works as an office admin for a social care provider.

### Sarah Hindmarsh (p. 47)

Sarah Hindmarsh is a private tutor by trade, and a writer in most of her spare time. She has self-published the award-winning 'Animal Adventures' series for six to nine year olds and the ever-popular '1001 Writing Prompts' series. She also has a growing collection of short stories and poetry published in various literary journals, magazines and anthologies. In her remaining spare time she walks her miniature poodle, Kohla and competes in showjumping and dressage (with significantly more success in the showjumping) on her horse, Callie. Sarah can be found on Facebook and Twitter.

**Jonty Levine** (p. 69)
Jonty writes fantasy and science fiction, largely as a distraction from pretending to be a grown-up. Perhaps for this reason he is often flitting from project to project, still currently working on his first novel. A Nottingham resident, but originally from Essex, he began publishing short stories in 2017, and seems to be making something of a habit of it. He of course thinks social media sites are the plague of a devil that must be destroyed, but you can follow him anyway at @JontyLevine on Twitter and Instagram.

**Keris McDonald** (p. 97)
Keris McDonald was born in Wales, studied Philosophy at the University of Durham and lives in Yorkshire with one husband and two dogs. She is a writer of horror and fantasy fiction and has been published in *Weird Tales*, *The Best Horror of the Year Vol.7* (ed. Ellen Datlow) and *Legends Vol.3* (ed. Ian Whates), among others. However, she spends more of her time writing erotica and romance – much of it with a fantasy or mythological theme – under the name Janine Ashbless, and can most easily be found online via www.janineashbless.com

**Angela Readman** (p. 11)
Angela Readman's short stories have won The Costa Short Story Award, The Mslexia Competition, and the Anton Chekhov Award for Short Fiction. Her story collection *Don't Try This at Home* was shortlisted in the Edge Hill Prize and won The Rubery Book Award. Her debut novel *Something like Breathing* was published by And Other Stories in 2019. She

also writes poetry. Her poems have won The Charles Causley Competition, The Essex Poetry Award, and The Mslexia Competition. Her folkloric collection of poetry *The Book of Tides* is published by Nine Arches.

### Louise M M Richards (p. 91)

Louise Richards is a retired academic, now creative writer and lives in Derby. She has been ably encouraged in her literary endeavours by the Derby branch of the WEA, her tutor, a close-knit writing group, good friends and family.

She has three grown-up daughters, all of whom she breastfed as babies at a time when 'bottle' was becoming increasingly popular. She often found this particular life choice difficult, but felt it was better for them and better for her.

She finds that writing is never purely a daily routine, but a way of life that has taken her comfortably into middle age and beyond.

### Marija Smits (p. 149)

Marija Smits is a mother-of-two, writer, editor and ex-scientist. Her somewhat eclectic writing has appeared in various places including *Mslexia*, *Shoreline of Infinity*, *Strix*, *LossLit*, *Literary Mama*, *Reckoning* and *Best of British Science Fiction 2018*. In spare moments she creates fantastical art. She can be found at: https://marijasmits.wordpress.com and on Twitter: @MarijaSmits

### Aliya Whiteley (p. 135)

Aliya Whiteley was born in Devon in 1974, and currently lives in West Sussex, UK. She writes novels, short stories and non-fiction and has been published in places such as *The Guardian*, *Interzone*, *McSweeney's Internet Tendency*, *Black Static*, *Strange Horizons*, and anthologies such as Unsung Stories'

*2084* and *This Dreaming Isle*, and Lonely Planet's *Better than Fiction I* and *II*. She has been shortlisted for a Shirley Jackson Award, British Fantasy and British Science Fiction awards, the John W Campbell Award, and a James Tiptree Jr award. She also writes a regular non-fiction column for *Interzone* magazine.

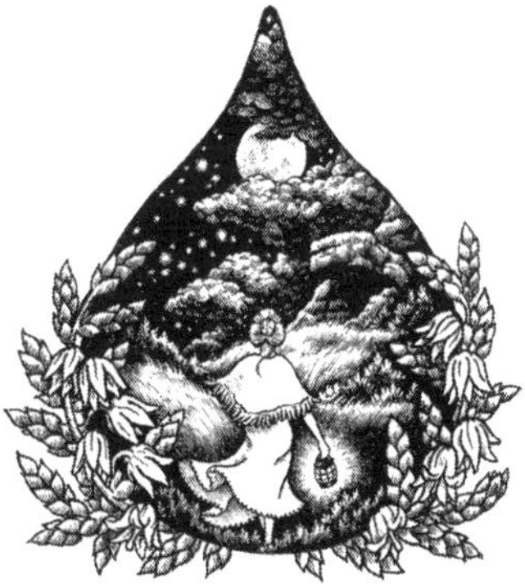

**Mother's Milk Books**

is an independent press, founded and managed by
at-home mother Dr Teika Bellamy.

The aim of the press is to celebrate femininity
and empathy through images and words,
with a view to normalizing breastfeeding.
The annual Mother's Milk Books Writing Prize,
which welcomes poetry and prose
from both adults and children,
runs from September to the end of January.
Mother's Milk Books also produces and sells art
and poetry prints, as well as greetings cards.
For more information about the press,
and to make purchases from the online store,
please visit: www.mothersmilkbooks.com